JINA S. BAZZAR

SPLENDOR'S ORBIT

THE MACLEE CHRONICLES BOOK 1

Copyright (C) 2024 Jina S. Bazzar.

This book is a work of fiction. Names, characters, places, and incidents are the product of the author's imagination or are used fictitiously. Any resemblance to actual events, locales, or persons, living or dead, is purely coincidental.

All rights reserved. No part of this book may be reproduced or transmitted in any form or by any means, electronic or mechanical, including photocopying, recording, or by any information storage and retrieval system, without the author's permission.

Cover design by MiblArt.

Splendor's Orbit

Chapter 1

I watched the two men strolling through the market from under my hood. Hands resting on my lap, feet propped on the stool, I looked like a bored vendor having a slow morning, though I was anything but. If the client didn't show up soon, I'd have to pack up and leave.

My stand offered a few secondhand items, things only the desperate and the broke would consider buying: ship components, used gadgets, some debris whose origins eluded me yet occasionally fetched a handsome price. There was even the holographic projection of a hull piece, since it was bigger than my four-by-four stand.

The salvaged items I found during my return trip from Astra-9 brought some income, as did the other items gained from other excursions. They kept my bills paid and food on the table, and allowed me to keep a low profile.

"You're watching those two?" asked Mac in my ear, the sentient AI who shared parts of my body.

"Mmm," I acknowledged. I wasn't surprised Mac had locked on to them. They'd been moving from stand to stand, eyes watchful, stance military straight. They were cautious enough to avoid brushing against anyone, despite the market being crowded.

They were no civilians. Not because they were dressed nicer than anyone in these parts dared to dress. Not because of the slight impression of the weapons they carried, concealed but not undetected. No, it was the predatory way they moved, a fluidity only rigorous training and experience could provide.

A second later, biometrics of the two appeared in my

right vision, courtesy of Mac. A torrent of information scrolled through the right side of my vision, with *Warning!* in bold lettering flashing at the top.

The two men were Kroz, the race responsible for peace and justice in more than half the planets in the galaxy—the kind of people I did not want to meet, no matter the circumstance.

Being peace- and justice-keepers gave the impression that the race was made up of nice, gentle people, but it was the complete opposite. They were ruthless, they were merciless, and they gave no quarter to rule breakers.

And I was the embodiment of a lawbreaker just by existing. If jumping up and running for it wouldn't scream guilty in their faces, I'd have done that the moment they'd appeared. As it was, faking nonchalance was causing me immense stress and spiking my adrenaline.

The market was getting quieter, the footpath less crowded by the minute. Individuals stepped away the moment they noticed the dangerous vibes the two Kroz were emitting. A woman caught the gaze of the taller Kroz and froze like a statue, then bolted in the other direction.

Tommy and Ben, two beggar boys possessing an eye for profitable targets, moved their way. They paused mid-step, jerked their shoulders, and about-faced to wherever they'd come from. I wondered if the horizontal pupils gave the Kroz away, or if the flight instinct was just a gut reaction everyone had around their race. Had the Kroz's hoods been down, people would have seen the tribal tattoos on their napes and avoided coming face-to-face with the deadliest race in the known galaxy.

Even the other vendors were looking anxious at their presence, and they had nothing to fear. I knew for a fact every vendor in this market was honest—working people trying to keep a roof over their heads and food on the table. I knew; I'd run a search on every single seller. I'd learned long ago, both as a soldier and as a fugitive, that it was easier to go unnoticed by living among low-key people. It was certainly better than trying to blend in on a crowded thoroughfare where corruption ran rampant and merited tighter security.

A strategy I might need to reconsider. The thought flashed in my head as the two Kroz continued gliding closer.

Please let them pass by. Please let them keep moving away.

"Uh-oh," Mac said, and the scrolling disappeared, along with the warning flash.

The two men split apart, each going in a different direction. The taller of the two—dark-haired, golden complexion—paused in front of my stall, eyeing a scratched radiator, while the companion—shorter, paler, with hair that gleamed like polished silver—paused a few meters to the left, his profile in view as he kept an eye on the crowd.

The designated watch.

Apparently, my stand had been their destination.

I'd been made. How or when and why wasn't the concern, not at the moment anyway. My muscles tensed, my breathing evened out, my flight or fight instinct barely restrained.

"I'd like to speak with Captain Lee," the tall Kroz said in fluent Universal, eyes a deep shade of umber.

I blinked. "Captain Lee isn't available," I replied slowly, stomach sinking. "Would you like to leave a message?"

"No. I need to see him. I was told I'd find him here, in this stall."

Him.

The Kroz didn't know. He wasn't here for me. "I'm sorry. Captain Lee had to take a run. If you leave a message—"

The Kroz leaned forward on the stall, bringing the smell of cinnamon and smoke and something enticingly masculine to my senses. He braced one hand beside the fiber-optic cable and looked at me through lowered lashes. To the casual onlooker, he looked as if he was examining the items for sale—not that there was anyone casually watching.

No one was, in fact. Everyone was doing their best to act as if they couldn't see the two. Probably secretly grateful that their stalls hadn't been targeted.

"You're not listening, female," he enunciated slowly, as if I was too dumb to understand the meaning of his words. He looked up, eyes direct. The color in his irises shifted from yellow to green and then to soft brown.

I wanted to squirm in my seat but made myself hold the intensity of his undivided focus. There were flecks of gold in his eyes and a faint shadow on his cheeks. "I have an appointment with the captain. He's expecting me."

His words were like a slap to the face. I almost flinched. The sound of creative cursing came from Mac. "That good-for-nothing Leo is going to regret this."

New trepidation dried all the spit in my mouth. "You're the client?" I asked. Mac was right. I was going to kill Leo.

The Kroz straightened, his point made, and inclined his head regally.

"Who sent you?" I asked, just to be sure. It wouldn't pay to murder Leo only to find out later he hadn't placed two Kroz in my path.

A grimace crossed over his face before he answered, "Mikey Pooh."

Mikey Pooh. That was Leo's code phrase all right.

I stood. "I'll get the captain. Please wait here." Without waiting for a response, I moved into the back, flipped the tarp separating my stall from the back alley, and turned right.

"Call Leo," I said to Mac under my breath as I beat a hasty retreat to the docks. Stats appeared to the right of my vision, the interface bringing up my contacts' list.

"Yo, Captain. Did the client get there yet?"

"You blazing moron," I hissed, glancing back to see if the Kroz had followed me.

They hadn't.

Yet.

"Do you know what you've done? What the client is?"

"Your ticket to a better place and a faster ship," he answered smugly.

I faltered but didn't stop. "No."

"They can pay you, Leann."

"It's not worth it."

"Listen to me," Leo rushed to say before I could disconnect.

It was the serious tone in his voice and the fact that I'd known him for years that kept me from ignoring him.

"They'll pay you whatever you ask for, and because they're Kroz, you'll never make a safer journey. No one will dare to cross the *Splendor* with them as passengers."

"Yeah? I want three thousand credits."

"They'll pay."

That brought me to a standstill. "What? I meant three thousand universal."

"They'll pay," Leo repeated confidently.

Mac squealed in my ear. "We can get the latest laser turrets and a new coolant rod for the FTL drive, a fabricator for maintenance and replacement parts, not to mention a new food synthesizer."

The temptation was there. I considered the upgrades to my ship, the luxury of good-tasting food without the hassle of creating it, but then I considered what kind of individuals would pay three thousand universal credits for a run.

Only desperate ones was the answer that came to mind.

I didn't need desperate Kroz on my ship. "I can't."

"They might be able to help you with your little problem," Leo added quietly.

I didn't think so. Not only because my "little problem" could call the wrath of the Kroz down on yours truly, but also because I'd never in a million years reveal my darkest secret to a Kroz. Not that Leo had any knowledge of my secret. He knew I was searching for someone I'd lost contact with a decade earlier. He didn't know my friend had been kidnapped by scientists experimenting with genetic modifications, or that I'd escaped said scientists, leaving said friend behind.

"Hard pass," I told him. "I'll never trust their kind."

"You don't have to," Leo said. "The Kroz have spies

everywhere. All their intelligence is uploaded to a shadow net called Gamat Com. Get me access to it and I'll get you all the Intel you need to solve your puzzle about your friend."

Not likely. The Kroz would never condone the experiments those scientists were doing. If they had anything on those labs, the scientists wouldn't be out there in the first place.

"I never heard about Gamat Com," Mac said.

I frowned. I didn't think Leo was lying, but this was the first I'd heard of it too. I had no doubt that now that we had, Mac would do his best to uncover everything he could about it. And his methods weren't all legal.

"I'm sorry, I can't. Convince them to find someone else. And get your butt off that chair and go pack my stand. I left everything there."

I disconnected and hurried to the docks. The *Splendor*, my freighter ship, was docked in the lower levels, where berthing was cheaper and easier for me to come and go. My clients were people with small businesses who couldn't pay for bigger, better-known companies. Refugees of the war between the Human Confederacy and the Cradox—families without enough money to afford better escorts from point A to point B. And people who didn't mind making their way to the lower docks. It wasn't like it was the dangerous part of the station, as many lower docks in other stations were. Despite its location on the edge of Confederacy Space, Station V-5 enjoyed a relatively low crime rate due to half of its population being made up of veteran soldiers and families with nowhere else to go.

I hit the lower docks running, instinct telling me to hurry, regardless that I hadn't been followed. People hurried on their way in both directions. No one paid me any attention. In this area, people were always in a hurry: to disembark, board, get the day's work done. If you were on this level, you weren't here for leisure.

My ship came into view the moment I hit an invisible wall and bounced off, falling on my ass. I was up in the next second, poised to fight, hand close to my hip where my stunner pistol was holstered. But I could see no one.

That didn't mean no one was there.

"Engage infrared vision," I said sub-vocally, low enough that no one could hear it, but loud enough for Mac's interface in my right eye to engage and my right vision to change. There, a bit to the left where I'd bounced, the body heat of a person silhouetted in red, and another closer to my ship.

"We have a problem," Mac said. "The Kroz are here."

Chapter 2

Lord Drax

I stared as the female practically sprinted to the back, half amused, half annoyed. Kroz Warriors were formidable and unyielding, but it wasn't like we ran amok, killing indiscriminately.

"You hear that?" Thern, my second, asked as he paused beside me, gaze unwavering from the crowd still milling—the ones too curious, and the ones who had yet to notice our presence. "I think the female is fleeing from you."

I frowned at the dirty tarp where the girl had disappeared through. "Why? We have an appointment…" I trailed off, clarity setting in. "When your contact suggested we contract Captain Lee, did you run a check of their file?"

Those who ran from the Kroz for no reason usually were beings with nefarious deeds to hide.

"Of course. I even checked into the V-5 station log for the advisory board. Captain Lee is clean. No infractions, no misconduct, no criminal records. She's never missed a run or delivered damaged goods. She's got the best record too, in my opinion. If she relocates to the upper levels, she could even compete with the higher security escort ships."

I heard all that, but my mind had fixed on only one point. "She? The captain is female?"

My second canted his head to the side, though his attention never left the bustling bazaar. "Yes?"

I swore. "Void take you, Thern. Why didn't you say something?" I vaulted over the stand and jogged for the tarp-covered back. "That girl was our captain."

Splendor's Orbit

Thern followed me in. "No way. That girl is too young. Probably no older than twenty human years. The ship's advisory board showed a record spanning at least seven years."

That gave me pause. Then I recalled the cynicism and toughness around her stormy gray eyes that only hardship and experience could give. I pursed my lips. "You know better than to judge people by their looks," I chided as I drew back the tarp, only to find a narrow passage between stalls.

It was clearly a back alley that stretched to both sides—and currently empty of people. But I'd be damned if a simple human girl would give me the slip. Her footsteps had sounded to the right, and it was the right I took, inhaling deeply to parse the smells of burnt food, grease, motor oil, and unwashed bodies.

"I want all the information you can gather on Captain Lee," I told Thern. "All records you find, any newsclips—here or anywhere you can check without compromising our location, I want it."

"Sure," Thern agreed readily, falling in step behind me. "But why? If the captain doesn't want us on her ship, it would be better to find alternatives. We're already risking a lot by consulting strangers. It wouldn't be fun to be taken to a slave camp because the captain had a point to make."

I grunted. He was right, but we needed to get out of dodge without calling attention to us, and Captain Lee had been recommended several times when we'd put in discreet inquiries. *Reliable, skilled, asks no questions, and owns her ship.* Those were some of the words used. That and affordable. The latter wasn't a big issue, but the first four had been the combination I needed.

Our pursuers would easily predict our arrival at this station. I couldn't alter that fact. The next predictable thing to do would be to hire one of the best escorts out of here. That, I could circumvent. We wanted to evade capture, which meant we needed to do something unpredictable, crazy even by the Kroz's standards: board a freighter ship captained by a human. No Kroz would be caught dead aboard one, because no Kroz would put their lives in the hands of someone so inferior. Hence the certainty this captain would be taking us. It helped when Thern had confirmed the captain had a good record. The best, he'd also said. Discretion and safety were my only priorities.

"Where's Captain Lee's ship docked?" I asked.

"Lower docks." Thern conferred with his commlink. "The *Splendor* is on Level 6, Berth 33324."

"Switch to stealth mode. Maybe the girl wasn't the captain and she was telling the truth about fetching Captain Lee." No need to spook them in that case.

Thern scrutinized me. "You don't believe that."

I didn't. But I hadn't risen through the ranks by not taking improbabilities into consideration.

Chapter 3

I straightened and ran through my options. People weren't supposed to have mod-vision—no one was, unless wearing a visible gadget—but I didn't have it in me to act like I couldn't see the looming threat ahead.

My military background, though brief, had thoroughly ingrained an instinctual tactical approach to danger deep within me; it might as well have been coded in my DNA.

I eased my stance.

"Whatever you're thinking," Mac cautioned, his voice resonating inside me with concern. "It's not a good idea. You never have good ideas when cornered."

It was true. I didn't like to be cornered. But there was no time for anything dramatic because, in the next second, the two Kroz materialized, inciting some shouts of alarm.

Great, they're bringing attention to me.

No one wanted to associate with someone who had the scrutiny of the Kroz.

"Now it'll be doubly hard to get some clients," I grumbled, noting how people around us were edging away. I glared at the tallest Kroz, the one I'd bounced off. "You're causing a scene and ruining my reputation."

His umber eyes didn't even flick to the commotion around us, firmly focused on me. It was like he thought I was a threat that he'd pay with his life if he looked away.

"You're Captain Lee. I apologize for dismissing your status." He touched two fingers to his chest and lowered his head a fraction. "I thought Lee was a human masculine name."

I concealed a snort. He hadn't dismissed me because of

my name and we both knew it. Masculine and feminine were interchangeable, and not only with the human race. He'd dismissed me for my slight frame and diminutive stature. Standing at five foot two inches tall and looking like a stiff breeze could blow me over, I was used to being dismissed. More often than not, people's eyes glazed over me as if I weren't there. It suited me fine, so I never did anything to change it. On the contrary, I made my best to downplay my appearance. Unassuming clothes, posture, and no beauty accessories were my every day routine, intended to maintain an unobtrusive presence. Today, I had on dark cargo pants, a hoodie, and well-worn, scuffed boots. Dark, midnight hair had been braided to the middle of my back, and my hood obscured gray eyes that had been dubbed unnervingly intense.

"Look, I don't know what Leo told you, but I can't take you as my client. I'm sorry."

"Why not? I thought you piloted passengers. I'm a passenger, and I'm willing to compensate you for your service. You haven't even tried to negotiate." His eyebrows pulled together with genuine bafflement, as if the concept that someone would refuse him anything was beyond his comprehension. He wasn't insulted or aggressive, and that earned him points in my book.

I shook my head and decided to be truthful. Just a tiny bit. "I take you aboard my ship, word will spread around that the *Splendor* is a spy ship. I'll never get a job after that."

Understanding flashed in his eyes as he took in the fact everyone had paused what they were doing and were now openly watching us. Not close enough to hear, but close enough to tell what he was…and who I was.

"People come to me because they lack the funds to take other shuttles. I can't imagine a Kroz lacking funds, much less a ship of their own. There's no plausible reason for you to board the *Splendor*. I don't want the speculation that will come with that."

There was a pause where the Kroz considered my words.

To my surprise, he drew back, bowed his head, and motioned for his companion with a chin dip. "Very well, Captain Lee. My companion and I will retreat. We will return masked and speak again of my proposal."

Without waiting for my protest, both Kroz melted away, leaving me glaring at their retreating forms.

"I don't think we should wait for their return," Mac observed.

Me either. "Power up," I said as I closed the distance to my ship. "We leave as soon as the control tower gives us clearance."

***

"What do you mean they said no?" I snapped at the comms.

"There's been an incident, Captain Lee. No ship is allowed to dock or leave until the matter is resolved."

"I have an emergency," I began, but a silky voice interrupted me.

"Captain Leann," said Bloyre Muz, the Control Tower Supervisor. "Your insistence to leave when there's been a serious crime makes me wonder why you're in such a hurry. Oh yes, yes I wonder."

I cursed under my breath. I so didn't need Bloyre Muz's attention. Not now, not ever. He was a Cradoxian refugee who had applied and been granted mercy citizenship. Originally from Sector 9, the race locked in a war with humans on and off for more than a century, he'd fixated on me and my ship since the first time I'd docked on V-5. His relentless persistence was nothing short of maddening, and he had an uncanny knack for bullshitters. He'd tagged me as a liar the first time we'd crossed paths during my first cargo drop-off. Granted, I'd refused to let him poke his antennae into the cargo, and in response, he'd vowed to make it his life mission to uncover my clandestine dealings and see me behind bars. The fact he hadn't in seven years had made him unpleasant and confrontational. The funny part was that the cargo offload responsible for such animosity hadn't even been illegal. The irony was never lost on me. Since then, I'd taken pains to avoid him as best as I could. Most times, I'd been successful.

Today was not most times.

"I have a scheduled appointment to keep at Cyrus Station," I said, kicking myself for arguing with the control tower. "I don't want to be late."

"Uh-huh. You stay there until my men arrive. I want an inspection of the ship before you leave. Oh yes, I do."

"You can't do that," I protested, but I was speaking to dead air.

"Blimey," I muttered and pushed up from the pilot's seat. The thing about Bloyre Muz was that he wasn't wrong. Once upon a time, I went by a different name, and my current job skirted around the lines of legitimate and shady.

Stomping out of the bridge, I headed to the bunk area, mentally calculating how much time I had. Not much, considering Bloyre was like a snake, always laying low and ready to strike.

I had half a bunk-full of contraband to hide, the Control Tower Supervisor on my ass, and two Kroz to dodge. Today was not a great day.

I rushed to the cargo area, pulling a hover cart along to make relocation easier and hopefully faster. I had everything stacked in the next few minutes and was pulling the smuggled goods into the unused guest cabin when Mac spoke. "They're here."

Great. Fucking great.

I entered the small space, slapped the panel beside the unused closet, and inputted a series of codes on the inside panel. Three bleeps sounded before the wall to the right disappeared and a compartment appeared behind it. I quickly stashed the incriminating cargo, aware that station inspection personnel would start demanding entry any second.

Once done, I inputted the code again, then scanned my eyes. I waited long enough to make sure the wall had reappeared and that the compartment was completely hidden before

Splendor's Orbit

marching off to greet the most recent pains in my ass—the ones sent to sweep my ship for any proof of wrongdoing. My teeth ground together at the thought of how shitty this day was, and it wasn't even evening, Universal Standard.

Jina S. Bazzar

Chapter 4

Lord Drax

"You stay hidden," I commanded my charge as Thern and I approached the docks. "If anything happens, if you feel, hear, smell anything suspicious, you signal Thern."

My charge nodded and vanished from sight between one heartbeat and another. She had on a mask to prevent others from recognizing her, but people tended to remember two Kroz warriors and a masked girl faster and easier than two hooded figures traversing the lower decks of V-5 Station.

She had yet to master her Ashak, the gland responsible for the storing and the channeling of our energy. Her control was precarious at best, an anomaly for her line and her age. It was a vulnerability that others would try to exploit. I had no doubt she'd be a fierce ruler with or without Prime Magic, though the attack on my ship a few days ago told me not everyone was willing to wait and see.

Hence, the reason we were stranded in this backwater station without a means to go home.

I scanned the place where my charge stood, feeling the soothing ebb and flow of her energy output but not seeing anything. There was an odd solace in not witnessing the fear in her eyes for once. It was cowardly to feel relief at not being able to see her distress, but I was a warrior, ill-equipped to comfort the princess, much less a child. This would hopefully be over soon. If things went well, we'd be out of V-5 and en route home within the hour. Hopefully, our enemies were still sifting through the wreckage of *Wedva-Xa*, my destroyed ship.

Rage and remorse threatened to erupt within me at the

thought of my ship and crew, forever gone. I slammed the memory down and sealed everything into a mental box. It would be opened and let loose later when the princess' safety didn't take precedence.

Our first step was getting away from here. The pursuers would check V-5 Station, if for no other reason than it was the closest station to where we'd been attacked.

"You're sure she needs to do this?" Thern asked, gaze fixed on where the princess stood, unseen. "If Captain Lee makes us wait, she might lose control of her stealth form."

I gritted my teeth. The princess couldn't be seen, but she could see and she could hear. "She'll be fine. Our attackers don't know how many of us made it out in time, so they'll be searching for a girl. If all people see are the two of us, it'll buy us time."

Thern shot me a concerned look. "You still think it was premeditated. Our path wasn't broadcast for anyone to plan an ambush."

No, it hadn't been. On the contrary, only a handful of people had been aware of the journey, and even fewer had the knowledge of our route and timeline. But now wasn't the time to divert my focus. That time would come, sooner than later. Sooner, if we managed to convince Captain Lee to take us onboard her ship. Only then would I let myself analyze the implications of the ambush. Because it had been an ambush.

My gut told me the attackers had known exactly who was on that ship. They'd been too organized, the attack too swift. I'd barely had the chance to pack the princess into an evac pod and get the hell out of there.

"They were pirates," Thern said as we reached the docks. "I saw the flaming cross emblem."

"They were not," I said firmly. Pirates wouldn't destroy the spoils of conquest the way those attackers had. They knew our movements too well, their attack too precise.

My nails dug grooves into my palms, drawing blood. The pain only increased the anguish over my loss, but my resolve solidified; I was going to see the princess safe home, and then I was going to hunt everyone responsible.

I would not rest until I finished exterminating every single one of them. I wasn't dubbed The Grim Reaper for nothing.

"Nebula's breath," Thern whispered, then swore in Krozalian. "What the blazing void did you tell the control tower?"

I followed his gaze to find the *Splendor* surrounded by V-5 security personnel, complete with hover bikes mounted with weapons. All aimed at the ship.

I grimaced when I recognized Bloyre Muz, the Control Tower Supervisor—and Station Inquisitor when needed. "I told them that a crime had been committed against the crown and to lock down the station until we left."

Thern looked incredulous. "By the void! What did you do that for?"

"Because we arrived in an escape pod and anyone could have tracked that. I needed to secure the place to make sure we had enough time to arrange for transportation." My mouth flattened into a straight line as two officers strode down the ramp with clipboards. "I didn't tell them to detain the *Splendor*, though."

Thern's brow furrowed for a second before smoothing out. "You think the captain tried to leave?"

I didn't think. I knew. "Come on, let's go see how we can fix this."

Chapter 5

The sweep took hours. Hours where people, strange people, poked into my things, my private life, my ship, and I could do nothing.

Bloyre Muz himself had come, his antennae moving from side to side as he scanned my ship top to bottom, side to side. He'd arrived at V-5 long before I did. As far as I knew, I was the only human he was openly hostile with.

He was insectile in shape, scarecrow thin with a hard carapace on his back. He gave me the creeps, blunt teeth clicking as he scuttled about like an oversized cockroach.

After our first meeting, he'd been convinced that the *Splendor* was a pirate ship, and had never failed to jump at the opportunity to harass me. Even after I'd allowed him to inspect my ship, his suspicions weren't quelled. It didn't matter that there was nothing tying me to any of the pirate factions out there, he refused to entertain anything else.

Leo had once suggested I find myself a different ship, but I refused. The *Splendor* had been condemned for a chop station when I'd bought it for a song and a whistle. I'd upgraded the engine and renovated what I could afford. The signs of age and wear still showed everywhere, but I wouldn't give it up for anything.

Even after Bloyre scrutinized my registration and license for the umpteenth time and conducted a sweep of my ship, he still rejected the idea that I had an appointment to keep and needed to leave. To him, my need for speed could only mean I was hiding something nefarious.

He had an excellent bullshit meter. Yet, he'd never been

able to prove any of my documents were fake, and he wouldn't today either.

Amusing as it was, in the seven years since I'd first docked on V-5, I'd done my best to keep out of Bloyre's radar. Until today. And Bloyre had brought backup.

I couldn't help but think how with all his people devoting time here, whatever the crime responsible for the station's lockdown, his clues were getting cold by the minute. What an irony.

"Something funny?" Bloyre asked, teeth clicking as his antennae poised ahead of his narrow face.

I shrugged. "Just the fact that you have a crime serious enough to lockdown the station and yet here you are, devoting your best officers and wasting time on nothing."

"If you hadn't insisted on leaving so urgently, I wouldn't be here." Click, click, click, click. "It's my duty to investigate every suspicion, and you have raised the highest, yes you have." Click, click, click, his teeth continued.

"I told you, I have an appointment to keep."

Bloyre didn't respond to that, unless the click of his teeth had any meaning. Honestly, I thought he'd moved on from the conversation. It was perplexing that he lingered there, but I hadn't had many dealings with his race to know what was normal and what was not. I knew his insectoid race was a minority in the Cradox System, with the majority taking on a humanoid shape. I knew that his kind were fiercely loyal to one another, held grudges, and were emotionally sensitive. Beyond that, my knowledge was lacking. I was ignorant of their customs and traditions, or if they were herbivores or carnivores. Frankly, I hadn't wanted to know. My role as a soldier for the Confederacy meant I had been deployed to suppress skirmishes and intercept any Cradox ships attempting to breach Confederacy Space. It had been easier to fulfill my duty by categorizing the entire race as unthinking, unfeeling things.

For that reason, I couldn't tell if standing there on my bridge and fixating at a point doing nothing but clicking away was their way of relaxing.

I should have known better.

"Maybe you're the distraction put in place to divert attention and resources while the criminals escape. Oh yes, maybe you are."

"Oh, for fuck's sake. You didn't reach that position by being this stupid."

The clicks came faster this time, and I had a niggling suspicion they expressed his agitation. Click click click click. Bloyre stepped closer. "I can arrest you for slander, Captain Lee. You know I can, yes I can."

We were glaring at each other when the tall Kroz from the market stepped in, dressed in a long coat with the hood up. "That's enough, Inquisitor."

Inquisitor? My stomach did a nervous lurch.

Bloyre spun with an agility that told me he'd be a hard opponent. "Sir, I—"

"I heard. Thank you for your assistance. Recall your people and go."

"But, you don't understand. Captain Lee—"

"Is with me."

Bloyre clamped his mouth shut with a loud click. He lingered for a few moments more, his left antenna bobbing up and down. No doubt trying to come up with something else to accuse me of, but then he threw me a nasty look, antennae quivering with what I assumed was rage before he whistled and marched out of my bridge.

"You arranged that I be grounded," I accused the Kroz, fists clenched.

"Not really." The Kroz twitched a shoulder in a mock shrug. "This wouldn't have happened if you hadn't tried to leave."

I wanted to deny it, but it was true. "Is there even a crime?"

His eyes chilled. "Yes," he said curtly.

I wondered if the severity of the crime justified a

lockdown and if the Kroz had been involved. Of course they were. They weren't the universe's most notorious justice keepers for nothing.

The Kroz stalked to the co-pilot's seat and gracefully dropped into it. He was an apex predator who thought he had his prey by the neck and was looking forward to the meal.

Except this prey had claws and knew how to bite back.

"Now, Captain, let's discuss our arrangement."

I indicated for him to continue with a chin lift, not dropping my gaze from his. His irises contracted in reflex, and I wondered if, like an apex predator, holding his gaze was an invitation for challenge.

He angled the co-pilot's chair to better face me and leaned forward. The smell of cinnamon and smoke wafted from him, spicy and tantalizing.

"I need transportation for three to Krozalia. In exchange for your service and your silence, I'll pay you five hundred universal credits. You get a hundred credits bonus if you can make the trip without stopping."

"And if I say no?"

"I'll insist."

Would he force me, blackmail me, or steal my ship?

"Will I be breaking the law?" I asked, because I didn't miss the part where he was paying for my service and my silence. Not to mention he wanted me to take a three-months trip in one go.

The tightening of his eyes was the only indication that I'd insulted him. "No. I wouldn't ask that of anyone."

"Are you wanted? Carrying forbidden artifacts?"

"That's an insult to my honor."

"Are you?" I asked again, not looking away from his frigid gaze.

"No and no."

His answers didn't ease the nagging feeling growing in my chest. The one that told me danger was afoot, and it was time to dodge and run.

Splendor's Orbit

Why would a Kroz who's willing to pay a fortune come to me for travel? He could pay half that amount to charter one of the luxury ships.

I looked at the *Splendor's* controls from his point of view and couldn't come up with one good reason why he chose me. While the *Splendor* wasn't the oldest model out there, it was still not as sophisticated as most ships. No holographic consoles, state-of-the-art med units, or automatic food processors that produced gourmet dishes with the flick of two fingers.

And I wouldn't change any of it. My ship was simple, efficient, and didn't need a specialist on every corner to function.

"What's the catch?" I said, glancing back when the second Kroz stopped at the entrance to the bridge and crossed his arms. "Wait, you said passage for three. Who's the third person?"

"You're not going to believe this," Mac said in my ear. "There's a disguised kid in the cargo area."

"Intruder in cargo bay area," Mac's voice came through the intercoms, mechanic and without inflection. "Potential hostile. Intruder in cargo bay—"

"No!" the Kroz interjected, standing. "She's the third passenger." The second Kroz was already running. I contemplated the Kroz's broad back as he followed his companion out.

"Stand down," I said loudly to Mac for appearance's sake. My ship would never attack a kid, no matter what.

"What was the theatrical announcement for?" I asked.

"She was doing that invisible trick the Kroz employed earlier. Had her figure not flickered, I wouldn't have known we had a stowaway."

Mmm. "Is she restrained or injured?"

"Doesn't look that way. In fact, she had a good opportunity to run but hunkered down instead."

"Who are you?" I demanded when the tall Kroz returned to the bridge, his hood down. He had dark, even hair that looked glossy and thick. It was long enough to cover past his ears and the nape of his neck, where I heard all the Kroz had their tribal tattoo, but it wasn't long enough to be tied back.

He closed the small distance to the co-pilot's seat, stalking forward with a measured yet distinctly predatory gait.

"My name is Ravi Drax. My companion is Thern Boloski."

"And the kid is?"

"How do you know she's a kid?" Ravi Drax asked, though with curiosity, not suspicion.

Shit. "I checked," I said with a hand wave, then woke up the dark screen on the arm of my chair. An image appeared of a blonde child wearing a black mask and the second Kroz—Thern—talking earnestly in the cargo area.

Bless Mac and his ability to think for himself. Other AIs would have never been able to act without implicit commands. And the man in front of me was the reason Mac's existence was punishable by death.

"Who's she?" I repeated.

"My charge, Felicia. I'm escorting her back to her parents in Krozalia."

"Why the mask?" I asked, unsure if that was a societal thing or if it had a more sinister meaning.

Something flickered in the depth of his umber eyes, but I didn't know him well enough to decipher the meaning.

"Because I need to safeguard her identity from the public," he said slowly. "It's for her own protection."

"Says you."

Ravi inclined his head and motioned to his companion. A moment later, the girl appeared, hood down but mask in place. I studied the violet eyes with the horizontal pupils, the way she grasped her hands together as if nervous but willing to go through with whatever this was.

"You can ask her whatever you wish. She's not here under duress and I mean her no harm."

I motioned for her to come in. "Please, come on in," I said.

Without asking for permission from either Kroz, she moved in, pausing in the middle of the bridge. I glanced at Thern. "Do you mind stepping back and giving her some space?"

He raised an eyebrow and pushed off from the entrance. I pressed a button on the arm of my chair and the door to the bridge slid shut. I had enough time to see Thern's amusement fade to alarm even as I grabbed my stun pistol and pressed it under Ravi's chin.

The kid cried in protest but didn't come any closer. As for Ravi...I had no doubt had he not glanced at Thern when I drew the pistol, he'd have blocked me. It was not a nice feeling. Aside from looking irritated, he didn't seem alarmed at the turn of events. I didn't know much about Kroz physiology, but a direct hit to the head with a stunner was sure to drop anything, no matter how tough-looking.

"Felicia, right? Do you speak Universal?" For a moment, there was no response. I didn't dare take my eyes off the Kroz.

"Yes," came the tentative reply from the girl.

"Good. This makes things easier. Now, kid. Tell me. Are you here under duress?"

My eyes never left Ravi's. They had turned an improbable shade of yellow, the horizontal pupils more pronounced.

"No," she replied softly.

"I can get you away from them, Kroz or not. I will take you back home if I have to."

Something flashed in the depth of Ravi's stare. The yellow dimmed, making his eyes look warmer—was that approval? Respect? Maybe that was how homicidal looked for the Kroz.

"He's my uncle," she said, again gently.

Oh. "Being related by blood doesn't make him safe. I can call station security, your parents, or anyone else. I won't let him hurt you."

"Thank you," she said. "He's not my blood uncle; he's my Dradja. He's not going to harm me."

"Dradja? What's that?"

The kid was quiet for a few seconds. I didn't take my attention off Ravi, pistol steady.

"He's oath-sworn to protect me with his own life."

My eyebrows arched with surprise. "You'd die for her?"

"Yes," he said at once. No pauses, no hesitations.

I dropped my hand and tucked the pistol into the holster on my hips.

"Satisfied?" Ravi asked.

I grunted, sat back, and let the door to the bridge slide open again. Thern dashed inside, eyes scanning the three of us, presumably for signs of a fight.

"Stand down," Ravi said. "Captain Lee was simply making sure we meant Felicia no harm."

Thern scowled and hid whatever weapon he held. His hand didn't stray far from his side as he moved to stand slightly in front of Felicia. I ignored him and focused on Ravi. His eyes were back to that umber hue, expression guarded.

"Yes?" he prompted when the silence stretched. "Are you content now?"

No. Not at all. But I didn't know how to get off from this deal. "If I agree, it won't be to take you to Krozalia." I raised my voice when he began to protest. "I'll go as close as the nearest station, but I won't land in Krozalia." "The nearest station to Krozalia is Dupilaz Moon, and it's days away from the planet."

I shrugged. "Then that's as far as I'm willing to go."

Ravi's lips thinned.

"Look, that's my condition. You don't like it, find someone else." I put on my implacable face and waited.

I'd expected him to argue more, but after a very brief pause, he dipped his chin in agreement.

"Very well. We have a deal." "Not yet. I need to confirm you are who you say you are."

At that, Thern huffed in disgust.

Mac was no doubt running the names Ravi had

provided—his human name, considering the Kroz language was too convoluted for the human tongue. Something about extra vocal cords the human body lacked. In my early years as a cadet in the CTF—the Confederacy Task Force—I'd heard rumors about those extra cords being responsible for the magic the Kroz possessed, but nothing had been confirmed. They were mostly a mysterious race, their secrets guarded zealously.

I tapped a few keys on the control panel, again, for appearance's sake. My ship wasn't allowed to think for itself, the same way my enhancements weren't allowed to exist. Well, my ship was just a machine, but with the exception of the navigation controls, Mac had free access to the engines and always anticipated my needs.

"If your story is confirmed, I'll let you know now that my price is 3500 universal credits."

Thern scoffed. "You're crazy if you think we'll agree to that amount."

"Agreed," Ravi said.

His easy acceptance had me halting my tapping to look at him. He was serious.

"I also can't go into deep-space without making a stop first."

"It'll be best if we don't have to."

I nodded. "But I can't. I need provisions for long journeys." I brought up the Galaxy's wanted list and input Ravi and Thern's names.

"What if we can make the trip in half the time it usually takes?"

I paused tapping and looked at him. Unless he knew of a secret gateway, there was no way we could travel a three-month journey in half that time.

"Holy shit, he wants you to double jump the distance," Mac said.

Double jump was the term the military used for when a ship went from gateway to gateway to gateway without traveling in between. It was something the Confederacy had learned was possible right before my last mission. I had heard rumors here and there in the past few years but nothing concrete. I hadn't considered that the Kroz were capable of the deed, but I should have. They were the ones who had, after all, built the gates. Their technological advancement far surpassed that of humans by several centuries. I was more out of sorts than I'd guessed for not coming to that conclusion.

I pursed my lips. The knowledge would come in handy—even if Ravi tried to conceal the procedure, Mac could lock on to it. But I didn't think my ship could endure the strain the double jump would put on it.

The *Splendor* had never been a powerful ship, not even during its inception as a freight carrier for a transport company. Even if I factored in the upgrades I'd installed, it still wouldn't perform double, or triple jumps. It was in good condition now, but the engine was still a C2 class, meaning it could only undergo one jump safely without needing to cool and recharge. Maybe twice if we were desperate, but going from Sector 8 to Sector 5 would require more than two jumps.

"My ship can't—" I began.

"It won't be a toll on the ship, more like a shortcut," Ravi interrupted.

Mac inhaled a sharp breath. Not that he needed to breathe, but he liked to imitate human expressions. "That would be a handy thing to know. Say yes, please."

I cocked my head and ignored Mac's plea. "I've never heard of a shortcut."

"Have you ever been to the Krozalian System?"

Hmm. Good point. "Is this knowledge that will result in consequences later?"

"Not for you," Ravi replied.

Meaning someone else would pay. Him? Thern? Someone else higher up in the Krozalian government who'd divulged a secret they shouldn't have?

"Well?"

"Say yes," Mac hissed.

"My ship has enough provisions to keep me alive for a month. If I need to feed three more," I gave him a casual shrug. "You do the math."

"Fine," Mac said. "Just remember the opportunity you're giving up when we come across a new lead two sectors away and you realize you'll never get there in time."

"Thern can get what you need from here."

"I also need some parts for my ship, and I know what kind of parts they sell here. Unless you want to risk getting stranded in deep-space, I'll need to stop at a bigger station."

"You're such a spoilsport," Mac said. "Now, look what I found."

On the right side of my vision, information began scrolling.

"There was an incident near Salba two days ago," Mac highlighted the relevant information as he spoke. I turned to my screen and listened to Mac's report while going over the highlighted parts on my vision.

"The ship *Wedva-Xa*, roughly translated as Dark Sky, had some technical problems that led to some sort of engine malfunction. No survivors are listed yet, but an escape pod docked on V-5 two days ago, carrying three passengers. I'm running the pod's registration to see if it matches that of the ship."

I tapped absently on the screen and skimmed the information Mac had provided. It sounded plausible enough.

Mac continued, "I'm going to dig into Ravi Drax and his companion's identity and see what I can find about them."

"Fine," I said, returning my attention to Ravi. "I want a thousand credits upfront. You have two hours to get your things and get settled. We leave after that."

"We can go now," Ravi said, swiveling in the co-captain's chair to face out. "We have everything ready."

Chapter 6

The trip to Cyrus Station went uneventfully, with my passengers mostly keeping to themselves. The only two rooms they used apart from their bunks were the galley and the gym, though the kid rarely left her bunk, and never took off the mask.

The first thing the two Kroz had done when they'd settled was disable the surveillance in their cabins, which I let be. If they wanted privacy, I could give them that. I'd caught Felicia laughing and speaking freely with both Ravi and Thern, and deduced that not knowing the child's identity was for her benefit, a last layer of protection. It made me wonder who the kid really was.

I wasn't current with Kroz celebrity, but I had a feeling this kid ranked as one, or close enough. The fact she had her own security detail enforced that belief. Add in Ravi's assertion that she was important and the mask she'd refused to take off, even after we'd left the station, and I was ninety-nine percent sure. I was reserving that one percent until Mac could give me more on the trio.

I requested berth in the middle levels of the station, closer to Baltsar's Bits and Pieces, where I could find good, though not premium, ship parts for sale.

While docking at this level came at a higher price than I'd typically pay for a stay, the Kroz's need to not stop anywhere had me on edge. I figured paying extra was a fair tradeoff for an easier departure, so that's what I did.

I loaded my contraband on the hover cart for delivery, draped a dark tarp over it, and secured it in the cargo bay. My lips turned down at the knowledge that I wouldn't be able to deliver the smuggled goods myself. For a moment, I considered finding another passenger ship for the Kroz, but I pushed the idea away, albeit reluctantly.

I shrugged on my coat and headed off to find my passengers to see if they needed anything from the station. According to Mac, Ravi was in his bunk, and since my dealings so far had been with him, I tramped to the first bunk on the crew section—if I ever decided that I needed one. The next one was Felicia's, while the third was Thern's. I didn't miss the fact that they'd sandwiched the kid between the two. I'd have been surprised if they hadn't, actually.

I touched a finger to the scanner beside the door just as it slid open and revealed Ravi on the other side. Either he had great hearing or he was already coming out.

I drew back and looked up at him. It wasn't that he was too tall; he was average, no more than six foot tall. It still put him about a head taller than me. Yes, I was that short.

"I'm going out for a few hours," I said. "Do you need me to pick anything up for you?"

"No."

"You sure? It'll be a while before we stop again—"

"I'll get what we need."

That gave me pause, but I wasn't his keeper. "Okay, just make sure you're back on the ship in two hours."

I turned to go, aware of the looming presence behind me, and tried to ignore it. I grabbed the hover cart handle and pulled it along behind me. I inputted the code for the ramp to lower and we both waited as it did. I was aware of all the illegal things I carried and felt incredibly self-conscious. Of the man beside me, of all my illegal enhancements, of the stolen property on the hover cart between us.

Never had the ramp taken so long to lower, but the moment a gap wide enough had formed, I darted out—an advantage of being short and compact.

Without looking back, I let myself get lost in the hubbub.

Cyrus Station was one of the big ones; a neutral

metropolis, responding neither to the Kroz nor the Human Confederacy. It was a midpoint between two major gateways, and for that the station attracted a constant stream of travelers and tourists of countless races. It was also due to its prime location that one could find anything they wanted. From ship parts to exotic food—Cyrus Station had it all.

With the hood of my coat covering most of my face, I made my way through the docks and up two flights, with Ravi following behind like an insistent tail. That was fine. After all, most shops were located on the upper levels, and he did say he'd get what they needed himself. Still, his presence behind me made me nervous, not only because it attracted attention, but also because he was a Kroz. And a big one to boot.

Despite being mostly a trading station, Cyrus Station was still home to a large number of people. For that reason, the place was divided into quadrants, each with lower and higher levels, or decks, depending on who was speaking.

We were in the second quadrant, somewhere on the upper levels where the shops weren't cheap but wouldn't charge me an arm and a leg. I pointed out a few shops to Ravi so he'd know where to go, not bothering to tell him not to act like a tourist so he didn't get ripped off. Anyone willing to pay more than one thousand universal credits without haggling wouldn't care how much they paid in a shop.

"Groceries, clothes, gadgets." My finger moved from store to store as I indicated what they were. Ravi's eyes followed with interest. But he didn't move to any of them, so I continued on, pointing out to the other shops as if the Kroz was blind and deaf and couldn't hear or see the wares showcased by windows and the announcements being called.

"Coffee, plants, baby clothes, sex store."

Near the intersection that would lead me to Baltsar's shop, I came to a sudden stop and whirled.

"For fuck's sake. Are you going to keep following me around?"

"Yes."

Splendor's Orbit

I sputtered. Up until that point, I'd thought he was simply going in the same direction I was. It hadn't occurred to me that he was actually following me. Well, I did have a nagging feeling when he kept to my shadow like black on tar, but I didn't want to acknowledge it until I had no choice.

"What the blazing starlight for?"

"To make sure nothing happens to you."

I gritted my teeth. Be polite, I told myself. "I don't need a babysitter. You can go grab whatever you need for the journey."

"I don't need anything but the safety of my pilot."

I opened my mouth and closed it. He'd said that with so much sincerity, it rendered me speechless.

Mac snickered in my ear.

"No, thank you," I said at last. "You can go back to the ship and wait there." When the Kroz didn't move, I gestured with a hand. "Move on now, go."

"You're calling attention."

It was true. People were giving us sideways glances, some were even openly gawking. Ravi wasn't boasting his Krozalian heritage, but he wasn't hiding it either. Yes, he had his hood up, but if he'd wanted to go incognito, he could have put on some dark glasses to cover the unusual color and shape of his eyes. And there were too many people milling—and staring. It wasn't every day they saw someone arguing with a Kroz. Hell, they probably didn't come across many Kroz in this part of the galaxy. Cyrus Station was a neutral station, following no set rules but their own, welcome to all and any.

I ground my teeth and spun around, resuming my trek silently and hurriedly. The sooner I got the supplies, the faster I'd be back on my ship. If I could lose a particularly annoying Kroz on the way, points for me.

I reached Baltsar's shop a few minutes later, walking in and letting the door shut behind me, hoping it would slam on the face of a particular alien. If I were lucky, it would drop him unconscious until I was ready to leave.

The shop smelled of hot iron, new rubber, and engine oil,

but everything was well-kept and well-stacked. The boy behind the counter was new. He looked young enough that he should have been in some station-approved program for minors.

I moved to the back, having been here enough times to know what I needed wouldn't be out here on display.

"Can I help you?" the gangly teenager asked.

"Is Baltsar in?" I asked, not seeing the old man anywhere.

"In the back. Should I fetch him for you?"

"No," I said, pushing through the wooden beads separating the front of the shop with the workshop in the back, where engine parts were brought for recycling, dismantling, fixing, or whatever else Baltsar did with the spoils. I'd brought him enough salvaged items to know not everything was put up for sale, regardless if they were in good condition.

Ravi followed me in, and although it made me want to tell him off, I figured things would go a lot faster if I let him be.

At first glance, Baltsar was nowhere to be seen, but then I heard a curse and followed the low mumbles toward the back corner, where a pair of combat boots disappeared under a large engine.

"Pass me the wrench, will ya?" came the muffled voice from under the machine. I parked the hover cart, looked around, found a set of tools on a scratched table, and picked one up.

"Here," I said, crouching to hand the tool over.

There came a clank, a curse, and then Baltsar scrambled from under the engine.

"What are you doing here?" the old man demanded, glaring.

"Hello to you too. I'm well, thank you. I know, I know, it's been so long."

Baltsar's glare darkened. "What are you doing here?" he repeated.

"I need a spare energy boost for my FTL jump," I said before he could begin spouting words I didn't want Ravi to hear. "A new coolant, and all these parts." I handed him the e-pad with my notes, but he didn't even spare my list a glance.

Splendor's Orbit

"What's wrong with your FTL?" Baltsar asked with a frown. "It was in good condition last time I checked."

"Nothing is wrong. I need it because I'll be traveling into deep-space."

Bushy eyebrows lowered as he opened his mouth. Then Ravi moved, and Baltsar turned to where the Kroz stood, arms crossed.

"Yes?" Baltsar inquired politely.

"He's with me," I said.

Surprise flickered in the depths of the old man's eyes, but he didn't make any comments. Not aloud anyway, the look of "are you crazy" he gave me was loud enough.

"Are you being threatened or coerced?" he asked pointedly, and my heart melted a little for the old man.

"No. He's just my client's detail." It was something Baltsar would believe, and it was true anyway.

Or not.

Baltsar's hand shot out, grabbed my wrist, and tugged me behind him.

Ravi shifted, but I shot him a glare before he could follow, grabbed the hover cart, and let Baltsar lead me away.

Baltsar kicked open the door to his office, pulled me inside, then shut it again. "Why the hell do you have a Kroz Warrior with you?" he demanded harshly.

A warrior? Baltsar would know, being half a Kroz himself.

Oh, shit. I had a Kroz Warrior on my ship. Two, if Thern was one as well, which I assumed he was. But then my thoughts realigned. Bodyguard or warrior, they were both there for the kid's protection, not for me.

"Cool your jets," Mac chided. "Your heart rate just went through the roof. It makes sense that a bodyguard would also be a warrior."

"I didn't lie," I said to Baltsar. "He's my client's bodyguard."

Baltsar considered that for a few seconds then grunted.

"Tell me how that happened and have a seat. Since you're here, I want to check your vitals and mechanics."

I shuffled my feet. "I didn't come for a checkup. I don't have time."

"Then hurry up. It's been almost a year since your last, and you're traveling into deep-space. You're not going to make it back in time for your annual checkup."

Reluctantly, I went around his desk and plopped down on his creaky chair.

"I'd tell you if anything was wrong," Mac grumbled.

"I know," I said sub-vocally.

Baltsar grabbed a kit from the third drawer of his cabin and brought it over. While everything in the office was dusty, or crumpled, patched, scratched, or oil-stained, the kit was pristine, gleaming silver with polish.

Baltsar wiped his fingers on an old stained cloth before he unlocked the kit, pulled on disposable gloves, and a myriad of other tools that were probably never used to examine another human being.

"How do you feel?"

"The same." I brought the sleeve of my right arm up and folded it over my elbow, exposing the crook. Without a word, Baltsar picked up a small screwdriver-like tool with a needle head and inserted the dark tip into the vein before depressing the five-inch e-spike. I gritted my teeth when the whole right side of my body stopped responding to my commands. My right vision dimmed, not losing sight completely, but someone else would have needed thick glasses to see.

"Can you move?" Baltsar asked.

"No," I lisped and shook my left index finger in the negative.

"Good." With that, Baltsar picked a small handheld device and began running diagnostics and recalibrating my mechanical parts.

"Have you made any progress?" he asked as he began fiddling with the cybernetic interface of my right side.

I grunted my response with a finger shrug. Speaking with only half your face wasn't an easy feat.

And he'd have known if I'd made any progress. Chasing dark labs backed by an even darker organization with the funding to buy and blow up entire asteroids at will was not a walk in the park. It took time, it took focus, and I was only one person, and Baltsar was an old man. There was Leo and his vast networking empire, but there were a lot of details Leo was not privy to. Suffice it to say, I wasn't a trusting person.

"Did you check the rumors about Caltech Farms?" he asked.

I gave him a thumbs up.

"I take it you didn't find anything?"

I pointed to the hover cart and grunted.

Baltsar's eyes flicked to the covered contraband. "What's in there?"

"olen suf," I lisped.

Baltsar's eyebrows went up. He fiddled with the control in his hand, placed it beside me on the desk, and moved to the hover cart.

"What's this?" he asked, prying open one of the boxes.

"Stolen...stuff," I repeated carefully, glad the words came out exact.

"From Caltech Farm?" He shook his head and pulled up a vial, examined it, opened another box, and pulled a different vial. "Looks like high-grade medication. Who's the lucky beneficiary?" he asked, covering the boxes again with the tarp and resuming his seat in front of me.

"Odette."

Baltsar pressed a few buttons on the control and smiled. I waited until he realized I had a problem and watched his humor fade.

"How're you going to the convent to deliver the goods with a Kroz warrior in tow?"

"I'm not."

Baltsar narrowed his eyes into thin slits. "You gave

someone my address?"

I shook my index finger and gave him my most level look.

Baltsar scowled. "I'm not making the trip to the convent to play hero proxy for you." He tried staring me down for a few seconds, then threw his hands up, the right still clutching the control. "Fine. But you'll owe me for this."

"My ife," I lisped, but he understood the words, and knew how much I meant them.

I owed him everything. My ship, my identity, my life. Without him, I'd either be dead or a mindless body controlled by the dark organization I was doing my best to destroy.

Baltsar's expression softened. There were new creases at the corners of his eyes, more white than gray on his head. Before he could start spewing nonsense, I gestured for him to hurry up and finish the examination.

His gaze held mine for a few seconds more, conveying the words he wanted to say. Then he lowered his head to the control and resumed fiddling. Casually, he asked, "Have any more labs popped up lately?"

I raised two fingers.

"You checked them out yet?"

"Soon."

"When you come back from this run?"

I hummed a positive.

He stopped fiddling and leaned back to look me in the eyes. "Maybe it's time to let it go, Clara."

"Leann," I corrected him. I'd buried Clara Colderaro the day Baltsar dropped me at the door to Odette's convent to recover from the wounds I'd received escaping the scientists eight years ago.

"Fine. Let it go, Leann, please. This is bigger than you, bigger than us."

"Someone needs to stop them." I tried to say it in a way that conveyed the savage certainty I felt, but the words came out mangled and destroyed the effect.

"I know people," Baltsar began.

"No." I tried to scowl. Taking in the concerned wrinkles on his forehead, I explained, "I can't let it go. You know that."

"It's been ten years. If he's survived the explosion, the programming, and all the modifications, he won't be the same person you knew."

I said nothing, only gazed at the old man steadily. I understood his concern. I really did. I'd barely survived the explosion, barely survived all the changes done to me after that. I had a suspicion I'd died a few times—I knew my heart had stopped more than once during my stay in the labs. And I knew that had it not been for Baltsar, I wouldn't be here today. But if it hadn't been for me, Alex wouldn't have been caught by them.

Baltsar searched my face as if he could read my thoughts, and for all I knew, he could. He had a dash of Kroz in his blood and could work some magic—bioelectricity manipulation, or bio-electric kinesis, or BEK for short, which was the ability to manipulate electric currents in the body.

We didn't discuss that dash of something extra in his genetics, mostly because he'd confessed the ability after a night of drinking. The topic had never resurfaced, and sometimes I wondered if he remembered that night at all, or if he was intentionally avoiding the topic by pretending it had never happened.

Whether he chose to tell me or not, I would respect his choice.

He never talked about his past—Baltsar was always closed off about that. He'd been brought into the lab and had done his best to help me retain my humanity even when countless others had lost theirs, and for that, he had my undying devotion. He was my rock during the storm, keeping me above the water and helping me break free when the scientists realized I wasn't as brainwashed as they'd believed me to be. He'd fought for me like an avenging angel and, together, we had laid waste to everything and everyone in our path.

With a weary sigh and a nod, he leaned closer and

resumed his tinkering.

For the next fifteen minutes, Baltsar silently read and noted several equations through his device, grunting with approval each time it beeped with an answer.

"There isn't much difference since last year," Baltsar began as he deactivated and unhooked me from his devices. "But combining the past five years, you've aged a grand total of three months."

I inhaled deeply, wriggled my toes, clenched my fists, rolled down my right sleeve, and stood. "Anything else?"

"No, all your mechanics are in mint condition. If you have more time, I can check out Mac's casing."

"No," Mac hissed in my ear.

"I don't."

"I thought you'd say that," he said with a wry smile and stowed away the kit.

"So do you have what I need for my journey?"

"Not the coolant," Baltsar said, standing and pulling off the gloves. "But if you give me an hour or two, I can get you one. I have the spare FTL charge here. It's not new, but in good condition and it has enough to get you to Sector 5 and back."

Krozalia was in Sector 5, the only habitable planet in that entire system. There was no need to ask why Baltsar suggested a round trip to that sector, not with the warrior in the adjoining room. There was no way I'd be setting foot on that planet, but I didn't correct Baltsar in his assumption. My FTL drive should be enough to get me there and back. But I had learned if I wanted to travel alone without a crew that could fix things on the go, it was best to make sure I didn't run out of food, fuel, and spare parts that I knew how to change. It was a rule that had kept me safe in the past few years, sacred like gospel.

I helped Baltsar empty the hover cart, ignoring his grumblings about inspections that could jeopardize his license and good standing with the Black Court—the current rulers of Cyrus Station.

Ravi was standing where we'd left him, scrutinizing the

Splendor's Orbit

shop in a nonchalant manner that I knew was misleading. There was nothing casual about that guy, least of all his observation skills.

I handed the list of spare parts I might need to Baltsar. "Get me those items as well. I have some other things I need, but I'll be back to pick up everything in an hour."

"Captain?" Baltsar called as I turned to leave. "There's a conclave taking place this week. There're a lot of new faces around, and the local rats are scurrying about, trying to score easy pickings."

"What kind of conclave?" I asked, stomach sinking.

"Some sort of agreement between the Human Confederacy, the Cradoxians, and the Brofil race. It's not a big delegation, and although security has ramped up, it would pay to be cautious."

I inclined my head. Baltsar's warning wasn't about the local populace and their propensity for exploiting outsiders, it was for the increased security and what that meant for me.

"There was no public announcement about a conclave and an agreement," Ravi interjected.

Baltsar turned his gaze to him. "No, there wasn't."

I hesitated to ask more with Ravi listening, so I nodded and left the shop. *Damn it all to stardust and back again.* I had chosen Cyrus Station for its neutrality so I could avoid the Confederacy, and here they were, no doubt en masse and on guard.

Outside, I scanned the shop fronts and wracked my brain for the location of the nearest dry goods store that catered to the locals. A reasonably priced one. I couldn't come up with any. I could find my way through Cyrus Station no problem, but the shops were another matter. No way would I traipse around with a conclave taking place. The presence of the Human Confederacy meant the presence of the Confederacy Task Force, and although the chances that I'd meet someone I knew were small, I wasn't willing to risk it.

"There's a canned goods shop two blocks to your right,"

Mac said, anticipating my dilemma. "They're off the beaten path, look well stocked, and have good prices."

I pulled my hood lower and took the right, hurrying through the current of pedestrians and shoppers with newfound urgency.

Chapter 7

Lord Drax

I trailed Captain Lee through the throng of races, locking on to her hooded figure as the elfin female deftly maneuvered around the crowd and did her best to lose me.

I'd never been to Cyrus station before, but recalled when a few Kroz had been dispatched to investigate an incident a few years back. If my memory served well, Lord Obsidian, the leader of the Black Court, had solved the problem without the need for Kroz intervention. Nothing else had been reported since. Oh, I didn't think the station was sparkling clean. Crimes happened every day, everywhere, but no law, galaxy-wise, had been broken since. How did I know that? Because Kroz spies were everywhere. Some were directly employed by Krozalia; others found an opportunity to make quick cash by reporting. We paid several fortunes yearly to enforce the law.

"Groceries, clothes, gadgets." Captain Lee said, pointing a slender finger at the array of storefronts as if I were an imbecile who couldn't read Universal.

It was almost like she had things to do that she didn't want me to know. It made me damned curious, a feeling I hadn't expected to feel. Not because curiosity was a strange emotion, but because I knew she wasn't leaving without me—not while Thern and the princess remained aboard the ship. It astonished me, this urge I had to find out more about this female. There was something about Captain Lee that called to me, a tingling in my chest that made my baser self sit up and pay attention.

My gaze flickered toward the coffee shop, the aroma and the variety of blends piquing my interest, but not enough to leave her side. I trailed her to the next intersection, where the captain came to a sudden halt and spun around. I took a moment to admire the way anger had blushed her cheeks and the light of indignation in her gray eyes before forcing myself to pay attention to her words.

"…follow me around?" she demanded.

"Yes." I marveled at the way the light in her eyes darkened.

"What the blazing starlight for?"

"To make sure nothing happens to you."

"I don't need a babysitter. You can go grab whatever you need for the journey."

"I don't need anything but the safety of my pilot."

Her mouth opened. then shut without a word escaping. Some of the anger left her eyes, replaced by baffled confusion, as if the concept of protection was a foreign topic.

"No, thank you," she said. "You can go back to the ship and wait there."

I stayed put, taking in the three freckles on her right cheek and the way a muscle ticked on her right temple.

"Move on now, go." She waved a hand as if I was an errant pet dogging her steps. Amusement rippled inside my chest. No one had ever dared speak to me in such a manner. No one who cared to live afterward. And I couldn't help but find it…strangely refreshing. Here I was, feared by half of the galaxy, yet getting shooed off like a hound begging for attention by a slip of a female that barely reached my shoulders.

Attention that the captain was calling upon us. Normally, I didn't mind that, but my situation called for secrecy.

"You're calling attention," I said calmly.

I half expected her to stomp her feet and tell me she didn't care, but she glanced about, ground her teeth, and pivoted on her heel. She did stomp her feet as she marched away.

We continued to the right, heading into a quieter section, until we reached a shop with opaque glass windows. The sign embedded on the door in red letters read "Baltsar's" and nothing else. Nothing to indicate what kind of shop it was. No symbols or inviting lights that other establishments displayed to help attract customers.

I knew that kind of shop. It was the kind that catered to a very specific clientele.

The captain pushed open the door and marched inside without a backward glance. Not that she didn't know I was there. I assumed it was her way of telling me she didn't care if I was.

The shop looked bigger inside than it did from the outside. The smell of motor oil and engine fumes lingered in the air, along with something acidic and potent that brought me to a standstill and killed any lingering amusement: magic.

I inhaled deeply, but the other smells masked any identifiers. My eyes moved from stand to stand, taking in the gleaming ship parts and gadgets. I couldn't tell if the magic had been on someone or if it originated somewhere from the shop. Not because magic was illegal or anything, but aside from the Kroz, only another race possessed it, and the Levantines preferred to keep to their side of the galaxy. Despite the Levantines being versed in magic, only Kroz warriors had the ability to wield it and leave a trace in the ether. Any Kroz who unable to manipulate magic but still possessed it—called passive magic—considered it an additional sense rather than an active skill. Like the ability to feel someone's emotions, hear prominent thoughts in someone else's mind, understand their pets, and so on.

Although I lacked any evidence, I was almost certain that the attack on my ship had been orchestrated by another Kroz—someone who possessed passive, if not active, magic. Granted, I had amassed enough enemies to populate a small planet, and any one of them could have arranged the attack at a time when my attention would be solely on defending the princess. However, my instinct told me the timing of the attack had nothing to do with me and everything to do with the current line of crown succession—a position currently held by one teenage girl who had yet to master her Ashak.

I followed the captain to the back, where she was crouched talking to a red-faced man with graying hair and deep brown eyes.

Kroz.

Not a warrior and not nobility, not even a full-blooded one judging the round pupils, but someone with enough magic to leave the acidic imprint in the air.

Half-breed.

I inhaled, trying to parse the scent of the magic. The old man paused mid-sentence and looked my way. Our gazes connected and recognition sparked in his eyes. My teeth ground together.

"Yes?" he prompted.

"He's with me," the captain said, and the half-breed gave her an incredulous look.

"Are you being threatened or coerced?" the old man demanded.

Hmmm, he hadn't recognized me. Maybe that spark was the Kroz-to-Kroz kind, not the look-who's-here surprise look.

I watched as his hand snaked out, grabbed the captain's wrist, and pulled her further away. I'd have followed, but the captain shot me a warning glare that clearly stated not to. So I laced my fingers behind my back and tried parsing out what kind of magic this so-called Baltsar halfling possessed.

Chapter 8

"Why don't you make yourself useful?" I snapped at the hulking warrior behind me. "Go grab canned goods and whatever else you people would like to eat during the journey." I pointed at the aisle behind him. "Start there."

"Go, babe!" Mac shouted in my ear. "Show him who's the boss."

I ignored the urge to make a rude comeback. Not that Mac didn't know me enough to guess what I wasn't saying.

"I don't know what you'll need," he said, oh, so reasonably.

I inclined my head. "Consider my pantry empty. Now go."

Ravi gave me a questioning look, probably trying to figure out if I was joking, but then he pivoted and strolled down the aisles, gathering items as he went.

Things moved faster after that. I only cringed once at the exorbitant price I paid for all the food we'd grabbed. I didn't even haggle the astronomic price. Once everything was packed into the hover cart, we began retracing our steps back to Baltsar. Ravi seemed to have picked up on my uneasiness, because he continuously checked our surroundings, eyes alert. It wasn't that he'd previously been relaxed, or anything I could explain, really, but it felt like he was readying for a fight, as if his adrenaline was pumping higher and faster. Or maybe it was just my training kicking in, and the knowledge that the Confederacy could be anywhere on the station.

We were almost to Baltsar's door when a piercing alarm slammed my eardrums, and my connection with Mac died. Just like that. One moment, my link to him hummed softly in my mind, the next, there was nothing.

I didn't think. I didn't hesitate. I dropped the handle of the hover cart and bolted, pushing people out of my way when they didn't move fast enough. Behind me, Ravi shouted something that I ignored. I didn't have time to stop and explain. *What would I say anyway?* My AI's synchronization just went flat?

"Mac?" I said under my breath, dodging people and jumping over stationary carts. "You better not be pulling a prank." But I knew he wasn't. There was a vacuum in my psyche that was usually occupied by his presence.

The *Splendor* came into view, parked and unperturbed. People went about as if everything was fine. No one was gawking, dead, or screaming.

The only thing out of place was the airlock light blinking red, indicating decompression. I initiated the air pressure sequence, scanning the hangar for anything out of place as I waited. Not that the decompression was a normal thing. For one, I'd kept it pressurized when Ravi and I had left. For another, not everyone had the override code for an occupied hangar.

The moment the airlock light switched to green, I put in the code, then headed for my ship, eyes scanning.

Not seeing anything, I picked up my commlink and input the code for infrared vision. "Engage infrared," I commanded. Colors appeared in my right vision, some brighter than others, but nothing indicating body heat. "Engage ultraviolet," I said next, because I didn't know the visual spectrum for other races, and still, nothing stood out, even after a second lap around the ship.

"Mac?" Again, nothing.

The cargo ramp was shut, and nothing looked amiss. I moved around, searching, searching, searching…and found not one new scratch.

"What is it?" Ravi asked from behind me. He was hauling the hover cart with him. I couldn't bring myself to be grateful he hadn't left the provisions behind, my anxiety surging up a few levels.

I opened the panel at the rear, but the screen didn't light up or prompt me to input the code. I keyed in the override code anyway, ignoring the lack of beeps, and the red and green lights that should have followed. No locks disengaged, and no warning messages appeared. My stomach did a flip, a pirouette, then flopped again. My ship was dead, nothing but a big mass of hull and empty rooms. Panic was a hard ball in my chest, but I forced it back; it wouldn't help me find out why Mac and my ship were unresponsive.

My eyes swept the crowded docks. No one was acting suspicious, no one was looking alarmed, and there wasn't any commotion.

"What is it?" Ravi repeated, his eyes as alert as mine as he scrutinized everything.

"The ship is dead," I murmured. "Can you reach Thern?"

A muscle twitched in his jaw. "No," he clipped. "I've already tried."

That was when I noticed the commlink in his right hand. "Is that normal? You not being able to reach him?"

A crease formed on his forehead. "Occasionally. If he's resting or training or in a meeting, he might ignore my calls. But—" He hesitated, his uncertainty clear.

I could guess the words he wasn't saying: but this was an unusual situation, and he didn't think Thern would ignore him.

"Do you have another way to reach him?"

Instead of replying, Ravi touched his palm to the hull of the *Splendor*, eyes flashing yellow for a second before he flinched and stumbled back a step.

I didn't need to see his horror to know whatever had killed the ship and caused Mac to power down was nothing good.

"They're not here," he said, suddenly more alert than before, his body emitting a subtle energy. "There's nothing living aboard the ship."

"Do you have a way to track them?"

"You think I chipped them like animals?"

I ignored his sharp comeback and asked again. "Can you track them or not?" The possibility that they could still be on the ship, but dead, was not something I wanted to consider. Not yet.

Ravi bared his teeth in a snarl. "No, I cannot."

I headed out of the airlock and surveyed the bay to the left and right. Only a few minutes had passed from the time Mac's connection went dark, and whatever had happened to Thern and Felicia had to come after that. Instinct told me the two had been taken, but Cyrus was a big station. They could have been anywhere. If on foot, people would have noticed. On a vehicle of sorts, then. Something that could conceal a body or two.

I signaled to my left. "You search that way," I said to Ravi. A big hand closed over my wrist. Electricity zapped and I jerked.

Ravi let go quickly but didn't back away when I turned. "We shouldn't separate."

I shook my head. "This is a big station and we don't have the luxury to argue. We'll split up and cover ground faster." I pulled out my commlink and poised it in the air. "Whoever finds them first contact the other."

He passed his commlink against mine without arguing further. Without waiting to see if he had more to say, I dashed away, eyes searching. There, a guy with a small stand peddling protein bars and drinks for the departing and the arriving. I marched his way, pausing just in front of his collapsible stand, and turned around. He had a perfect view of the *Splendor*, depending on how many people were going by. But I was banking on the fact that he was taller than average. Probably born in one of those ill-kept stations with low gravity.

I motioned to the bar with chocolate and nuts—the most expensive of the bunch. "How much is a box of that?" I asked in Universal.

The man stood straighter and eyed me suspiciously. "Ten universal credits."

"How many do you have?"

Now he looked me over, no doubt taking in my generic clothes and sturdy, non-designer shoes. "Why?"

"I'll buy them all—if you can tell me anything about that ship." I pointed at the *Splendor*. "Anyone come in, how did they look? How many came out, were they carrying anything?"

"And if I've seen nothing?"

I shrugged. "I'll buy nothing and let you know the authorities will be heading this way soon."

"You gonna call them on me?"

"No, but I need to know what happened on that ship. I'll call them to investigate."

The man bit his lip, looking indecisive for a few seconds before he straightened to his full height and nodded. "I have eight boxes, plus the opened one. What about the beverages?"

"If you give me valuable info, I'll buy everything."

"One hundred and eighty credits. Universal."

I gritted my teeth. "Fine. And don't bother fabricating any tales, because I'll know."

The man tapped on the commlink around his wrist, then extended it to me. I reached out and scanned his chip, then authorized the money transfer for a hundred and eighty credits.

The man made sure I'd really transferred the money before giving me another assessing look. "A few minutes ago, three men paused by the airlock pad, pressed something against it, then walked in. I only noticed them because the third one stayed behind and kept looking around. The other two came out with a crate, one of those used in the export yard."

"What was inside it?"

"I don't know. It was sealed."

"How big?"

The man placed his palm about waist height. "This tall, and twice the size of my stand."

I frowned down at said stand. It was big enough to fit both Thern and Felicia, but it would be tight and uncomfortable. "Export yard?" I asked instead. It didn't matter if one or both had been taken.

The man pointed. "There's a big export yard about a hundred meters that way. Export goods from Cyrus are delivered there for inspection prior to departure."

My body urged me to run that way, but I forced myself to ask more. "Is that the direction they went with the crate?"

"Yeah, that way," he confirmed, pointing again. "They seemed in a hurry."

"Thank you." I turned and ran, ignoring his calls about the protein boxes and the drinks.

Ten minutes had passed since Mac's connection went flat. Whatever had been done for that to happen, it would still have taken at least two or three minutes for Thern and Felicia to be incapacitated, stacked inside a crate, and a few more for them to reach the yard. Whoever took my passengers wouldn't be running, because running called attention, and they didn't seem to want that. Otherwise, they wouldn't have bothered to conceal my passengers, much less do whatever they'd done to my ship.

Pros. Those people knew what they were doing.

I reached the export yard a minute later, and without hesitation, climbed the first crate tower I found, easily finding footholds and divots. Orders for me to climb down reached my ears. I ignored them, too busy scanning the sea of crates, jumping from one stack to the other. If only Mac would…what? Wake up? I had no idea what could possibly have been used to disconnect him not only from the ship, but from his main matrix on my wrist.

Before I was halfway into the yard, I spotted three figures dressed all in black pushing a big crate on a hover cart. I shouted a wordless order, but only one glanced my way. He had a mask covering his lower face—no, a snug bandana, like the ones worn in mining planets to keep the miners from inhaling too much powdered minerals.

I jumped to the ground and rushed to where I'd spotted them turning a corner. In hindsight, I shouldn't have made my presence known, but no one had yet invented a time machine, and I never shied away from the consequences of my actions.

I burst into the spot where I'd seen the three mercenaries just as something long and flat whizzed my way. I had enough time to duck and prevent my brain from making a mess of the crates, but not enough to dodge the hit completely. The flat bar hit me on my right thigh with enough force that had it been my left, I was sure the bone would have broken. As it was, impact and momentum carried me headfirst into a stack of crates. The sound my cranium made was loud, ringing both from inside and outside and producing the image of spinning stars and blinking red lights. I bounced back and fell, but had enough sense to roll away just as a large magnetic boot came down where my head had been seconds ago. I climbed to my feet in a move that should have been agile and graceful, but was little more than a flop and scramble. I dodged a gloved fist from one merc, a kick from another, and tackled the merc trying to make off with the crate. It cost me another hit to my lower back with the flat bar. Pain radiated from the impact in rippling waves, but I kept going. Partly because of physics, and partly from my long-ago military training. The merc I tackled lost his balance and fell atop the crate, and I followed with a muffled thud as it broke open and an assortment of legs and arms spilled out.

Someone grabbed my braid and rolled it around a fist before yanking. I scrambled to all fours, then upright to alleviate some of the pressure. The third merc grabbed Felicia's limp body and threw her over one shoulder, her hood falling in the process.

For a second that felt like an hour, I froze, one foot raised, ready to stomp on the foot of the merc holding my hair like the bridle of an equestrian pet.

Son of a bitch! I knew that face. Comprehension flooded my system like a splash of freezing water—swift and with the same refreshing clarity. Ravi's need for silence, the mask, the bonus offered for not making any stops through the journey.

My passenger wasn't a celebrity, and her name was not Felicia. No, her name was Dolenta Tsakid, and she was the Krozalian princess. My passenger was the daughter of Emperor

Rokoskiv, the most powerful person in the galaxy.

The question of how, why, and when circled my brain even as I stomped the foot of the mercenary behind me with all the strength of my mechanical leg. Bone crunched and the merc let go with a howl of agony as he dropped to the ground. In the same move, I kicked the next merc who tried to grab me—and missed when he jumped away in the nick of time.

I spotted the princess propped against a stack of crates, still unconscious, and too late, I realized I'd lost count of one merc. The flat of the bar hit me on the back of the head with so much force that I was out even before I hit the ground.

Chapter 9

When I next opened my eyes, I was alone in a graveyard of shattered crates. Getting back to my feet was an exercise of will, but I managed. My head pounded mercilessly, but I knew that had it not been for my enhancements, that blow would have killed me.

I forced myself to move, to not give the mercenaries time to get far. I refused to let my passengers be stolen from my ship, especially now that I knew who that passenger was.

Ravi and I were going to have a hard talk when I found my quarry. I'd probably kiss the three thousand credits goodbye too, depending on his explanation. I didn't want, and couldn't afford, now more than ever, the scrutiny my cargo would bring on me. But first, I had to find the princess. If I lost her now, nothing aside from a stellar implosion would keep the Kroz from descending upon me, and if I made it to Dupilaz Moon, I'd still be inundated with Kroz scrutiny.

No, thank you very much.

"Have you seen anyone suspicious pass through here?" I asked a guy lounging against a stack as I exited the maze of crates.

A shrug was the only response I got.

"Do you speak Universal?" I tried again.

"Do I look like a cheche?" the man demanded.

Cheche were small, blind rodents native to Cyrus Station. They became disoriented whenever they found themselves somewhere unfamiliar. They scuttled around, hitting their heads on walls and rolling around as if the world was ending. In reality, they were simply getting used to the new space and the feel of that space against their small bodies.

"They have a kid with them. Possibly wearing a hoodie."

"Like them ones you wear?" the man asked.

"Maybe. Have you seen anyone?"

"Depends." The man eyed me up and down, assessing me.

"How much?" I asked.

"One credit."

I motioned with my hand and he pulled out the cuff of his shirt, exposing the cracked interface of his station-issued commlink. I pulled my commlink from my pocket, passed it over his wrist, and deposited a credit.

"Now, tell me. What did you see?"

"Naldo!" the man bellowed, and a kid, probably no older than seven, stepped into view from behind a few crates.

"Tell the lady what you saw."

"Three Brofils carrying a man and a girl."

Brofil. Weren't they supposed to have blue-tinged skin? I hadn't been examining their skin color when I was fighting them, but that was the kind of thing that should have stood out. Hadn't Baltsar said there was a conclave going on between the Confederacy, the Cradox, and the Brofil race? My heart skipped. This was getting more complicated by the minute.

"Where did they go?" I asked.

"That'll cost you more credits," the boy declared.

Fury spiked inside me but I pushed it down. I didn't have time to argue—or throttle any sense into their heads. I motioned for his commlink and he raised a bonny wrist with an intact, but outdated interface. I deposited another credit. The boy pointed toward the adjacent building. "They went into Salas."

"We've alerted station guards," the old man told me with a crooked smirk.

My left eye twitched. I refrained from cursing. Not because I'd paid for the information when station guards were on their way, but because now I needed to get back my cargo and out of dodge before station security found the princess and rounded up everyone for questioning.

Never in the seven years since I'd started my escort business had I missed a delivery, damaged my cargo, or even lost it. And here I was, having my most precious cargo to date stolen from under my nose.

I burst into Salas Saloon, a typical-looking watering hole for the tired and the weary workers and travelers. The place was packed, loud, and smelling of sweat, burnt oil, and alcohol. I pushed my way inside, getting pushed back, but no one really paid any attention to me.

"Engage face recognition, recipient, Thern Boloski."

Nothing happened.

Stars, I thought as I pulled out my commlink and engaged the interface. "You better not have broken my friend," I muttered. Had Mac been online, I wouldn't need to use the commlink to give my right vision commands.

"Engage face recognition, recipient, Thern Boloski," I repeated the command and the right side of my vision came alive with flickering profiles as my implant tried matching Thern with the people I could see. I pushed my way into the back, not finding Thern, much less a child. But if the kidnappers had come this way, they hadn't come for a drink or a snack. I was too short to scan past the people, so I grabbed a stool and climbed atop it. There was a narrow stairway leading up, and a dim passageway half blocked by the stairs. I jumped down and headed that way, hesitating by the first tread to the second level. The passage behind the stairs probably led to an exit, but I couldn't fathom the reason why the kidnappers would take this detour when the crowd would have slowed them down. Not to mention, that many people, someone could have tried rescuing an unconscious child from being carried off by Brofil mercenaries.

A survey of the crowd told me if that person existed, he or she was not here. No one seemed ruffled, concerned, or alarmed.

Unless Naldo had lied.

A high-pitched laugh had me looking to the side, where a

scantily dressed woman was being led away by a short man. He pushed the people in his path, punched a guy on the shoulder, and took the stairs up to the second level. At the landing, he hoisted the woman over one shoulder, slapped her ass, and disappeared from view.

My eyes narrowed after them. Felicia—Dolenta, I corrected myself—could have been brought in carried bridal-style, with her hood up. Her size could have given some pause, but unconscious as she was, she wouldn't have been struggling, and there were plenty of people shorter than me in the galaxy. That would have meant Thern had been taken through some other way. But my main concern was the child, not the Kroz warrior.

All that flashed in my head in a handful of seconds. I glanced up the stairs and made up my mind. I climbed two steps at a time, pausing at the landing to a slim hallway with four closed doors.

I'd barely taken a step when hissing sounded in my ear, followed by a piercing stab in my brain. My right vision flickered, then Mac's voice sounded. "Well, take those suckers. Someone is going to pay for that!"

"Mac," I breathed, eyes stinging with unshed tears. "What happened?"

"Some EMP beam," he said indignantly. "Can you believe that? Someone shot the *Splendor* with an EMP beam in the middle of a freaking floating station!"

"Thern and the kid?" I asked, half hoping he'd tell me they were still on the ship and that those Brofils had been duped somehow.

"They're not here. I don't know how or when they left, but I can engage station security and see if I can follow their trail from there."

"Yes."

"How long was I out?"

"A little over fifteen minutes, no more than twenty."

Mac grunted. "I'll make those assholes pay. Do they even

care that EMPs are dangerous on stations that depend on keeping their power on to function?"

"You seemed to be the only ship affected," I said. "No one else back in the docks was alarmed or put off."

"Why are you in a brothel?"

As if on cue, someone moaned from behind one of the closed doors, and I realized a rhythmic thump was coming from another. I grimaced, but I put my ear to the door to my left, and when I heard nothing, kicked it in. A typical room greeted me—one large bed with a red and cream bedspread, a small boudoir, and mirrors on the ceiling and behind the bed. No one was inside. I kicked in the door of the last room, expecting to find it empty, and almost got shot in the head when the merc whose foot I'd pulverized shot me with a laser pistol. I ducked just in time—or so I'd thought. Red-hot agony radiated from my left shoulder. I hit the ground on the injured side, rolled, and was up again in no time.

"Who's that?" Mac demanded.

I ran for the stairs. "The distraction," I said between my teeth. Not because the wound on my shoulder hurt, even though it did, but because fast healing always skewed my concentration. Whether that was an unavoidable result of the scientists' tinkering, or a side effect of not finishing the enhancements I was supposed to have, I didn't know.

I narrowed my eyes and forced myself to pay attention. "There are two more Brofils," I said. "One carrying the kid, the other Thern. I don't know if they split, but the kid is their target. She's the Kroz princess."

I ducked into the passageway behind the stairs, mostly tuning out Mac's expletives, then hurried out the exit door into an alleyway.

"Got them," Mac said a moment later. "Two hooded people heading east of your location. One is carrying Thern while the other has the child. They're together, and people are giving them a wide berth. Hurry, their lack of discretion means nothing good."

I took the left and ran, following Mac's instructions and directions. "Where am I heading?" I asked.

"Mid-station ahead," Mac said. "Factories and the old hub, some residential units for locals. Take the right and the alley in the middle. I think I know where they're going."

I increased my speed, jumped over a few boxes waiting to be unloaded, and tried not to panic. People intent on kidnapping usually made for the docks, not away from it. If the station initiated a lockdown, there was no way the Brofils would escape with the princess. Not if they meant to keep her alive, anyway.

I ran down a busy thoroughfare when Mac indicated, slowing my speed so that I wouldn't stand out more than I had to.

"I'm going to send Ravi a text letting him know where you are heading."

I grunted.

My surroundings slowly changed from the civilized, touristy veneer to a more utilitarian front as I followed Mac's directions.

"How far is Ravi?" I asked.

There was a second while Mac scanned the station feed. "Not far. About four minutes if he comes running on the same path you took, nine if he keeps his current pace and path."

"Have him run, then. Where to?" I asked, looking to both sides of a busy platform and finding nothing amiss.

"Straight into the alleyway across from you," Mac instructed, and I ran, slowing to avoid stepping on the spilled contents of an overturned cart. This wasn't a nice section, but there was no need to be rude.

"How's the shoulder?" Mac asked.

"Itching and burning like acid."

"Mending well, then," Mac noted.

I mumbled an affirmative.

"Gotcha!" Mac shouted with triumph. "They've moved into the warehouse district and disappeared into a storage facility."

Mac led me to the facility in question. There was a side entrance, a requirement for any establishments to have in case of emergencies. I debated taking the front but decided on subterfuge instead.

"Can you get the lock?" I asked Mac, pressing my wrist to the keypad. The motherboard implanted in my wrist was Mac's main housing, the result of the year I spent in a bioengineering lab and the reason our connection went bone deep.

Mac made a scoffing noise in my ear. "Kid's play."

In a few seconds, the lock went from red to green. I caught a glimpse of a dim corridor before there was a flash of light and the world turned into heat and dust and debris.

Chapter 10

Lord Drax
I headed in the opposite direction Captain Lee took and scanned the faces I passed. I kept signaling Thern, but he didn't answer, and there were too many people about for me to search for energy traces in the ether. It had been easier to examine the ship since only Thern and the princess should have been inside, but the ship was empty.

They could be dead, said the voice inside my head, but I refused to believe that.

Thern wouldn't have gone down without a struggle, and if a fight had happened, I'd have felt the lingering burst of violence in the ether. Violence always left a strong mark behind. It took longer than a few minutes for that mark to fade away.

Come to that, even the princess would have fought tooth and nail. She might not have mastered her Ashak yet, but the kid knew how to protect herself. I knew, I was one of her instructors.

No, my second and the heir to the Krozalian throne were both alive. I wouldn't believe anything else until I saw evidence to the contrary with my eyes. Eyes that I knew were glowing and apparently conspicuous enough that more and more people were noticing me. It didn't matter. The time for subterfuge had passed. We'd been found, and the princess was missing.

I kept my energy at the ready, taking advantage of people's fear and the path they cleared for me.

The station got busier the farther I moved, not everyone getting out of my way as fast as I wished them to. I stopped suddenly. Instinct and logic told me that whoever had taken them would run for a less traveled path, not a busier one.

Splendor's Orbit

Cursing, I pivoted and retraced my steps, reaching the *Splendor* a mere minute later. I didn't see the captain, and I hadn't expected to, not after I'd seen how fast she could run. I paused by the airlock, closed my eyes, and tried again to detect the princess or Thern's energy and was surprised to find Captain Lee's instead. I opened my eyes and focused on the feel of her signature, the vibrancy and vitality that was uniquely hers. Finding the captain's trace in the ether in the middle of all the others was much easier than I'd expected.

Probably because she has so much life in her, she outshines everyone else. The poetic analogy of my thoughts brought me up short, causing an unfamiliar and uneasy feeling in my sternum. I shook myself mentally. This wasn't the time to dwell on the jumbled enigma that was the captain.

It took me another moment to parse the captain's trace in the ether and lock my senses on it. Within a minute, I had tracked the captain's steps into a yard of stacked crates, three tall and more than a dozen wide to either side. There was a commotion already taking place, along with angry demands for answers. I followed the raised voices to a multitude of broken crates where the captain's signature took a turn for the violence I had expected to find back on the ship, had Thern and the princess resisted their captors.

"This is a restricted area," a human in a blue uniform said, blocking my view of the blood and debris.

Since the captain's signature continued on, I didn't argue or ask questions. Instead, I tracked the trace into a saloon, where the signature divided into two. The one leading up was the same as the one leading in, but the one leading to the back had a darker hue, as if the captain was in deep pain. Something had transpired up there. I didn't have time to check upstairs when her traces indicated she had left through the back. I headed out the back, though something inside me wanted to go up and make sure that whoever, whatever, had caused the captain's pain suffered an agonizing death.

In the back of my mind, I knew my reaction was not

normal. Not that being able to distinguish someone's energy signature from another was.

It wasn't. Far from it.

But now wasn't the time, or the place, to contemplate the ramifications of either.

I had just turned a corner when the communication link in my hand gave a signal.

Thern, I thought, but instead, it was a locator address from Captain Lee, a small map showcasing the captain's current location and the best way to reach her.

I clenched my fist around the commlink and ran. This time, people didn't simply move away from my path; they screamed when they did.

The beast in my soul basked in their fear, and the glare in my eyes increased with the thrill of the hunt.

I spotted the captain disappearing into a dark doorway just as the whole place blew up.

Chapter 11

My vision was hot and red. No, the facility was on fire. I hadn't fallen far, mostly because with a wall behind me, there wasn't far to go. A large piece of the metal door covered my body, protecting me from the flames, but not the heat.

Mac was shouting in my ear, panic and static muffling his demands for me to get up, to move move move. The urgency in his voice, more than the words, had me groaning and shifting, pushing myself with both feet to slide from under the metal door that had no doubt protected me from a worse fate.

"Stop screeching," I muttered, and Mac's demands grew in volume.

"They're doubling back to the docks. Up. Up! UP! Everyone is converging on the warehouse district and the perpetrators are escaping in the chaos."

That had me moving faster. My head was pounding according to my heartbeat: fast, hard, and erratically. "They're Brofils. Can you find anything about them? Identity, the ship they came in on, if they're part of the conclave Baltsar mentioned?"

"Already on it. Now get up and move!"

A crowd had gathered on the periphery, no doubt breaking station protocol to step back and allow the experts to take care of the crisis. It was to no one's benefit when parts of a space station started blowing up, especially when the nearest planet was days away and evacuation wouldn't be an option for everyone. It told me that whoever these people were, they were viciously ruthless. I would bet my next salvage that they had been hired by someone who hadn't specified how they wanted the job done. Had probably insisted they did whatever it took to ensure the job's success.

It made me wonder, if the Brofils got caught who would deal with them first: their employer or the station authorities. My hunch told me whoever hired them would have a contingency plan in place for that exact event, but I didn't have enough puzzle pieces to form a coherent image yet.

"Why is no one trying to stop the people carrying a kid and a Kroz Warrior like thieves?" I grumbled.

"They're in a crate," Mac explained. "The two Brofils burst out of the warehouse driving a conveyer with two crates."

I skidded to a halt. "How do you know they're the quarry?"

"They're the only ones moving away from the warehouse district."

"It could be a decoy to distract me while they get away in the other direction."

Mac was silent for a moment. "I don't see anyone running from that direction smuggling a kid and an adult Kroz warrior. Besides, the two getting away have the same build as the two you've been chasing and they don't know they're being shadowed via station feed."

"If you're wrong—"

"I'm not," he interrupted.

"That's mighty arrogant of you," I huffed even as I dashed through the throng of gawkers.

A hand closed around my elbow and I whirled, fist first. I pulled my punch a fraction of a second before it connected with Ravi's stomach. Momentum made it impossible to prevent the impact, but at least there wasn't much oomph in it.

The Kroz Warrior grunted but didn't double with agony, so points for me. "What happened?" he asked, scanning my singed clothes. "Are you hurt?"

"Not the time." I yanked my arm free and resumed running. Ravi fell in step beside me.

"You know where they are?"

"I have a suspicion."

"Turn right on the next block," Mac said. "There's a blind spot there. If they know this station as well as they seem to, they'll make a stand there."

I veered to the right and Ravi followed, not asking anything else.

"You'll enter the blind spot in three, two, one…"

We burst into a big area, larger than I'd have guessed for a blind spot in a station of this size. Inactive machinery and ship parts were stacked haphazardly here and there, amidst empty hulls and more crates. The station's junkyard. I had this niggling suspicion this wasn't usually a blind spot.

I slowed down. Beside me, so did Ravi. He took a few steps away, giving us both maneuverability space.

Mac swore something filthy about a monkey and a banana that was probably impossible. "Someone found me out. I've just been booted off the station feed. You think I can't push my way in? I'll show you who's the daddy."

"Forget it," I said sub-vocally. "Make sure the ship wasn't compromised and get us ready to go the moment we board."

"I can do both."

"No. Don't risk getting caught."

Ravi was almost halfway through the area when the attack came.

Our assailants came fast, low, and in greater numbers than expected—there were more than two…more than five, and shifting so that I couldn't get an accurate count. All of them were dressed in black, with their hands gloved and a bandana covering the lower half of their faces.

Oh, good. More mercenaries.

"Do you think they called for reinforcements," Mac wondered, "or do you think this was the plan all along?"

I grunted and ran into the melee. I took the first punch and the second before I could avoid a gloved fist to the face that would have no doubt punched out my lights again. The merc I was fighting was tall and broad, but that was all I could tell. I backpedaled, only to find myself grabbed from behind. I jabbed my right elbow and kicked the one in front, and although I did no damage, I managed to free myself and put some distance between us. A third man jumped me from the left, and I rolled away, flinching when my shoulder impacted with the ground. The injury had knitted, but it could still open. I was barely upright when a wide torso tackled me to the ground again and I fell, face-first.

All my air left my lungs in one strong whoosh. I kicked back, hit something solid, and pushed sideways until I was free. I climbed to my feet—in time to be grabbed from behind, yet again. More mercs had arrived.

"Geez, woman," Mac remarked. "Where's all that fighting prowess you keep bragging about?"

"Need. A wall," I hissed under my breath. I needed something solid behind my back, or maybe to move closer to Ravi. Ahead, another man prowled my way. He had on all the black-on-black wear, but his face was bare of the bandana. His mouth turned up in a menacing grin, his canines long and sharp. I caught the bluish tint to his white skin, more prominent around the mouth and eyes. A well-fed Brofil, to make the blue tint so faint. No wonder I hadn't caught it with the three mercs I'd tangled with earlier.

I struggled to free myself. In response, the merc holding me pulled me harder against his body. I grabbed his wrist, pressed against the pulse point, and elbowed him with the other. His grip loosened, just a bit, but the one in front had reached us. I kicked him in the balls.

Hard.

With my right, mechanical foot.

I swear his eyes crossed as he went down, clutching his crotch and wheezing for air. "That's it, Captain!" Mac cheered. "Kick their ass—ur—balls."

Before the merc behind me could do anything else, I stomped on his foot. I slipped away the moment his grip was loose enough. That was the beauty of being small and underestimated—no one expected me to know how to hold my own in a fight, much less to come out on top.

I caught the gleam of a pulse blade in my periphery and ducked. I was still straightening when I kicked the merc's knee, then climbed his body, using the bent knee as a foothold. I punched him on the side of the head and flipped away, falling into a crouch and sweeping the legs of the next merc out from under him. He went down with a surprised gasp, and I was on him in the next second, pummeling his face with my fists.

"Mmm," Mac said. "Usually, Brofils run in packs of fours. Their fee starts at one thousand universals."

"Stop researching. Have you run diagnostics?" I asked sub-vocally, punctuating each word with a punch. "Focus on the ship, not me or the mercenaries."

Movement to my right had me rolling away and coming face to face with another Brofil. Too late, I saw the pulse blade in his hand, already on a downward trajectory. I threw myself sideways, the blade grazing my forearm and aggravating the throb from the earlier shot. I ignored the pain for the moment and knifed my legs up, pushing the Brofil into Ravi, who grabbed his head and twisted. One twitch of his hands and just like that, the lights in the Brofil's eyes dimmed. The body fell limply to the ground, neck crooked to the side.

My distraction cost me. Ravi shouted something I didn't understand. But I did feel the presence behind me. Before I could turn or move, something heavy and hard hit me in the back. I fell like a rock, only the strength of my right arm keeping me from breaking my nose on the hard ground. I was rolling in the next second, but the merc had anticipated the move and pinned me down before I could get far enough. Strong hands encircled my throat and began squeezing, the face of the merc above me coming and going out of focus. I tried breaking the vice-like grip around my neck, my mind stuck on how easy it had been for Ravi to break that Brofil's neck, and how lucky I was that this merc wasn't as powerful and that my neck wasn't as fragile. But

I couldn't break the hold, and the merc seemed impervious to my struggles. If he kept this up, it wouldn't matter how strong the merc was because he'd suffocate me to death. I scrabbled to find something to use, remembering the stun gun in my fake pocket. I grabbed for it, pressed it against his side, and held down my finger on the trigger.

It took a few seconds, but finally, The Brofil convulsed, and the hands around my throat loosened. I choked in a grateful breath just as the merc collapsed atop me. Before I could push him away, someone's foot kicked the stun gun from my hand. A strangled sound of pain escaped my ravaged throat as the gun skidded away and hit something with a loud crack.

"You think we should merge?" Mac offered, even as the ache of my fingers began dulling.

"Not yet. Anything broken?"

"Dislocated phalanges. I'm blocking your pain receptors until you can pull them back in place."

I hissed and pushed the body off of me in time to see the piece of a hull the size of my bed flying out of nowhere—straight at two Brofils closing in from my left.

Ravi was fighting off three others. He spared a brief glance my way and my whole body locked down at the feral look in his glowing yellow eyes.

"Get her out of here!" he shouted, then made a sharp motion with his hand. A Brofil I hadn't noticed creeping behind me flew into a strange machine with bone-cracking force.

Energy. Ravi was using telekinesis to fight. I didn't know much about the magic of the Kroz, but I knew not everyone could manipulate energy, and that those who did were powerful—and part of the ruling family. I also knew that the more energy a Kroz threw around, the weaker he became. From the way Ravi was throwing Brofils and engine parts around like a kid in a tantrum, I had a feeling he wouldn't be able to hold them for much longer.

The conveyer Mac mentioned with the two crates was parked closer to Ravi, behind more mercs. To get there, I'd need to clear the path. I grabbed my right hand, the sight of crooked, broken fingers making me nauseous. Trusting that Mac had dulled the nerves enough, I flattened it above my belly and rubbed my fingers quickly into place. The pain of the realigning joints was there but faint.

I opened my mouth to tell Ravi we'd deal with the mercs together, but then I saw them: eight more mercenaries had arrived. Were they all Brofils? It didn't matter. There were at least five on the ground, seven more still up, and the princess was the priority. The right thing to do would be to grab the princess and bolt.

But I've never been the kind of person to turn the other cheek or keep moving while someone lay bleeding on the ground.

If I were, I wouldn't be here today. Not freighting cargo back and forth, not trying to pass as someone I wasn't, much less fighting a gang of Brofil mercs with God knew what in mind.

So I dove for my stun gun, rolled as I grabbed it, and came up firing. I had downed three mercs before I realized the weapon had been set to lethal and all three mercs had a fist-sized hole in their chests.

"Well, that answers the question whether you followed my instructions correctly," Mac mused.

I gritted my teeth. "I shouldn't have let you talk me into tinkering with the stun gun."

Blind spot or not, the lethal discharge of a projectile weapon would have been picked up by the station's scanners. In a floating station where a small hull breach would cause everyone's death, banning projectile weapons was a no brainer. I'd never been to any station that hadn't always kept their scans calibrated to the highest setting.

Cursing, I took cover behind a boxy thing with wheels and tried to set the pistol back into non-lethal stunner mode, but found the makeshift switch stuck. I recalled the crack I'd heard when the merc had kicked it from my hand and cursed again.

It was one thing to be involved in a fistfight. Another to

leave unconscious bodies on the ground. And something else entirely to leave dead bodies behind. Not that I'd never done any of the above, but damn it all, I didn't want to kill for the Kroz.

Not that I was seeing many choices ahead. Those mercs were here to do business, and if that business included getting rid of me, they'd do it without hesitation. Between my life and theirs…there wasn't even a choice to make.

I sighted the next mercenary and pulled the trigger. By the time Ravi and I were the only two people left standing, the space was filled with bodies, most dead, some unconscious. I was sure that if we managed to escape Cyrus Station before security caught up to us, we'd never be coming back. I spared a brief thought for Baltsar and our yearly appointment, then left my hiding spot.

The adrenaline spike had ebbed and I was feeling every second of the past thirty minutes. Ravi wasn't fairing any better, though he wasn't bleeding anywhere I could see. His skin looked wan and clammy, his chest heaving as if he'd been running for days. I guessed using his telekinesis had cost him. Hopefully not so much that he couldn't make it back to the ship.

Chapter 12

I looped Felicia—Princess Dolenta's—arm around my shoulder and hurried as much as I could without looking like I was dragging a half-conscious girl through the station.

Ravi had stayed behind to see if he could find any quick clues about who had hired the mercenaries, promising he wouldn't be far. By then, both Dolenta and Thern were coming out of whatever drugs they'd been given.

But even without dragging the princess, people were noticing me—not only was I injured, but my clothes were singed and ripped. And when people noticed that, they took the extra second to look at the person beside me. Even hooded, there was no mistake that I was half-carrying a barely conscious kid.

When people began stepping away and clearing a path around me, I knew they weren't trying to help but to distance themselves from whatever punishment was heading my way.

"Are we ready for takeoff?" I asked Mac.

"Unauthorized, sure. I'm hacking into the tower mainframe to get the hatch to open."

"How long will it take?"

"It'll be done in time for our departure."

I muttered a curse under my breath. Unauthorized departure, explosions, and dead bodies. Even if Cyrus Station didn't put a reward out for me, the *Splendor* would be on every wanted list out there. It would be a pain changing name and registration to something with a background strong enough to withstand scrutiny. I could already envision the three thousand and five hundred credits I'd make on this run going to all the repairs for the damage caused to my reputation and ship.

Of course, that all depended on us actually making it out of there.

Yes, Ravi and the princess could clear the air as easily as a wave of a hand, but I was another matter altogether. Besides, if they had wanted to announce their presence, they wouldn't be paying me to transport them to Krozalia.

"This is why I keep a low profile," I muttered when the princess stumbled and went down to one knee. A man shouted for me to step away from the child, but he wasn't wearing station guard uniform and didn't try to approach us.

I crouched in front of the princess and adjusted her hood with one hand, the other firm on her shoulder, preventing her from landing face-first on the floor.

"Look at me," I demanded harshly, and she blinked dazedly for a second too long. I squeezed her shoulder. "Look at me, Princess."

Purple slit eyes met mine, still glazed from whatever drugs she'd been given.

"I'm going to get you home, do you understand me?"

The princess blinked again.

I bit back impatience. "Do you want to go home?"

"Home," she breathed.

"That's right. I need you to concentrate. The ship is near. Can you make it?" I squeezed her shoulder again. "Can you make it?"

"Yes."

"Good. Now, I'll help you move. Just try not to fall."

I pulled her up again, but I could tell we were already too late.

"Ravi just cleared the blind spot," Mac said. "But security is closing in from ahead and your right."

"I see them," I acknowledged, grunted, looped my arm around the princess' middle, and practically picked her up.

The *Splendor* came into view ahead. Unfortunately for us, the security guards were closer. Six of them against one. It wasn't impossible odds, but I was already tired, bruised, and those weren't thugs with nefarious plans. They were security guards for the Black Court, the insignia of a black throne gleaming darkly on their chest.

"Station guard," one of the men called in flawless Universal. "Unhand the child, then step back. Slowly and carefully."

I inhaled. "She's my charge," I called to the guard, figuring Ravi wouldn't mind my claim if I was able to de-escalate the situation. "We were ambushed and she got hurt in the process. Now I'm simply trying to get her to the med bay of my ship."

"Step away," the same man shouted.

I considered my options just as six more guards arrived, dressed in dark blue and white uniforms.

The Human Confederacy uniform.

While I was certain Ravi could clear everything up with Cyrus Station security, the Confederacy Task Force was another matter altogether. I wasn't exactly wanted by the CTF, but only because they didn't know I was alive. And I'd rather keep things that way.

I tensed, ready to fight my way through, then reassessed. If I left a trail of bodies on Cyrus Station that included security personnel and Confederacy soldiers, I'd never escape far enough from their justice-seeking vengeance.

But then Ravi took the choice from my hands. A concussive boom sent everyone flying off like blown-away pieces of cardboard. Though I'd have rather he didn't do that, I wasted no time. I threw the princess over my shoulder and ran for the airlock, inputted the code, and without prompting, the ramp for the *Splendor* began lowering. To outsiders, it would seem like a crew member was operating the ship, but if Ravi or Thern noticed that, I'd have a lot to answer for.

I moved up the ramp and rushed to the bridge. I didn't have time to settle the princess in her bunk, so I plopped her into the small emergency bench, hooked her up, and fell into the pilot's seat.

"How close is Ravi?" I asked.

"They're entering the airlock. Security is shouting for them to stop."

"The hatch?"

"Ready to malfunction."

"Coordinates?"

A series of numbers appeared on my screen. "We'll need to hop the moment we're here," a small light appeared on the screen, some distance away from the station. "It's the closest spot we can safely hop from. The trick will be dodging traffic and evading any hostiles the station launches before we reach the spot."

I pursed my lips. Hopping was what people called small jumps done without the assistance of a gateway. It would cost us energy, probably increasing our journey by weeks or even months. Unless we made another stop for an energy boost for the FTL. After what just had happened, I didn't think another stop would be wise.

But it wasn't like we had any choice.

"Have the shields ready to engage the moment we're clear of traffic."

"Done. Ramp is closing. Should I melt the clamps or break them?"

I scanned the screen, thinking fast. "Break them." It would probably cause some difficulties if we needed to dock, but melting would tip the station off that the *Splendor* had some weaponized tricks. I didn't plan to get caught fleeing, but if it happened…well, I'd rather have some things left up my sleeves.

Make plans for your backup plans, my instructor in the academy used to tell me.

"Decompressing the airlock," Mac announced through the ship's intercom.

That would buy us some time while at the same time starting a countdown. The tower could override the decompression, as well as whatever Mac had done to take control of the hatch.

Splendor's Orbit

What a fucking mess.

"We're launching. Grab on to any handles," I said through the intercoms. The ship lurched as we broke the station's clamps, and a second later, the engines engaged and we dashed off.

I allowed my mind to touch Mac's matrix, just a light melding to help me think faster and navigate through the other incoming and outgoing ships without losing speed, aware that we were being hailed by the station, the com's light blinking furiously.

"I spot three patrols." Mac linked my mind to the ship's control panel, and my image field expanded, then contracted on three red pinpricks, coming from my left, right, and rear. I maneuvered around two arriving ships and increased speed. I just needed to clear transit nearest to the station, then we'd go full thrust to the spot where Mac had calculated a safe hopping point.

"Two more ships were deployed," Mac stated, but they were far enough behind us that my main concern was the first three closing in. They were encumbered by the traffic as well, though, so the matter was more about who the better pilot was.

Not to brag or anything, but I'd been one of my father's best pilots even before I had joined the military at eighteen.

"Target lock," the ship's intercom alerted.

Ravi dropped into the co-pilot's seat and belted in. His hands flew over the console, and the ship who'd locked onto the *Splendor* came into view. It was the ship to our left, and it was the one with the clearest line of sight. But shooting us with this many ships around wasn't a smart move, not even if they were the best pilot with the best ship. Any damage caused to the *Splendor* could send us careening into a second ship, then another, and no doubt more. Either the target lock was a scare tactic, or the patrol would rather cause an incident than let us escape.

Unless, of course, the patrol ships weren't part of the station guard.

That question was answered when Ravi engaged the

coms.

"Ship 24680 titled the *Splendor*, this is Captain Jacobs from Cyrus Station. Surrender or we will shoot."

"So eloquent," I muttered, engaged the thrusters, dropped sideways, and swooped beneath a large tourist ship. Ravi sucked in a startled breath, and glared at me. Not that I was looking, but I could feel the hot scorch of his disapproval on my face.

I didn't blame him. Putting a tourist ship filled with innocent people between you and a ready-to-fire ship was a dick move, but I was confident Captain Jacobs wouldn't shoot.

"This is the *Splendor*," Ravi responded into the coms. "We have diplomatic permission to leave the station. License 343B, Section 3C Code Locust, Omega, Transit, Ferris, Alpha. Accordance Hail Mary with Lord Obsidian."

My eyebrows shot up so fast, they would have hit the ceiling had they not been attached to my face.

The comms crackled and hissed. "You will surrender and be released if found innocent," Captain Jacobs repeated.

So much for special permissions.

We left the more congested traffic behind and I was about to engage full thrusters when a cruising ship to my left suddenly locked on to the *Splendor*. No, not a cruising ship.

A Human Confederacy Class 3 battleship, I realized when I finally saw the golden emblem on the nose. The kind that came complete with turrets, laser mounts, and a platoon of stealth ships ready for deployment.

***

The boarding clamps sounded like a gong in the silent bridge, the thunk thunk thunk of magnetic locks jostling the entire ship before stabilizing again.

Without a word, Ravi and I undid our harness and stood. While he went to help Thern from wherever he'd secured him, I headed to the princess and helped her unclip her harness.

There was fear in her eyes, but she didn't ask me for reassurance. Either she'd been well trained, or she understood there was nothing I could do. Probably both and more that I

Splendor's Orbit

didn't have the time to think about.

By the time the airlock was cycling, the four of us stood, as ordered, waiting for our captors.

Ravi and Thern both stood slightly ahead of Dolenta and me. Their stance was mostly casual, but I've seen Ravi fight and kill with a hand twist and knew how deceiving the posture was.

The first person through was a forty-something black man taller than Ravi with a standard stun gun ready and aimed, and various other weapons strapped to his person. Two men flanked him, both white, younger, and carrying the same amount of weapons as their captain. They were dressed in Cyrus Station security attire, but the people in the back had on the CTF uniform. Thankfully, the trio blocked my direct sight of the Confederacy soldiers, and theirs from me.

The black man and his two companions stepped forth, and my attention snapped back to him.

The variety of medals gleaming gold on his chest told me he was a high-ranking official, and his name tag read Cpt. Jacobs.

His eyes moved over the two men then back to me and Dolenta. She was clutching my arm, head lowered, hood up.

"Who's the child?" Captain Jacobs demanded, taking a step forward.

My impression of him went up a notch. People usually tended to dismiss children and deal with the adults, but unfortunately for us, it was clear his priority was Dolenta's safety first.

Dolenta flinched and stepped back, and Ravi took a menacing step forward. "She's my charge." Captain Jacobs gave Ravi a once over, no doubt taking in the blood—that was probably not even his—then he did another assessment of the four of us. "And what's a kid doing with someone like you?"

I didn't think he meant it as an insult, more like what's a kid doing with a Kroz warrior covered in blood, but the Kroz took offense. Ravi growled, an honest-to-God animalistic sound that rattled from his chest, and suddenly there were three weapons pointed at his head.

Someone at the back gasped, and a familiar voice called a name I didn't think I'd ever hear again.

"Captain Colderaro."

The man to the left of Captain Jacobs was pulled back and a familiar blonde man took his place. "My God," he said, face paling. "It's you."

"Hi, Sunny," I said with fake cheerfulness. "Fancy seeing you here."

It was during that distraction that Ravi attacked. Or that's what I surmised happened. At least one weapon discharged, and there were simultaneous grunts and thumps. I didn't even see who moved first, but suddenly Ravi had Captain Jacobs by the throat, while the captain's stun gun was pointed at Ravi's chest. Thern was convulsing on the ground with another guard's stunner on the back of his head.

The third guard stepped in and came for the princess.

Ravi's snarl was ferocious, accompanied by another growl.

"Oh, crappety crap." I pulled Dolenta behind me and backed away a few steps. "Sergeant Sullivan," I said through gritted teeth. "Call off the guards before they cause an intergalactic incident."

I didn't think Sullivan had the authority to call off the captain, but I was hoping he could talk some sense into the other men. A look at the captain's red face and bulging eyes told me he wouldn't be able to do this alone. I licked my lips and said, with all the authority my one-time position had granted me, "Captain Jacobs, you're assaulting Princess Dolenta Tsakid's bodyguard. Stand down."

Chapter 13

Lord Drax

I stared down Admiral Fulk, biting back all the vicious remarks I wanted to make. "I'll graciously accept the two stealth fighter escorts, but the princess, I, and my second will continue on the *Splendor*."

"Of course," he said placatingly. "I just wanted to emphasize that we have more capable pilots and better ships at your disposal than a deserter facing court-martial, pending an investigation."

Dolenta glanced up at that. Though her expression looked serene, I could see traces of alarm in the glow of her eyes.

My ire at the admiral's biting words rose with vengeance, though outwardly, nothing showed. I touched the princess' shoulder in reassurance. I wouldn't let this admiral do anything to Captain Lee.

Captain Lee, or Clara Colderaro, was one of the best pilots I'd ever met, as shown by her demonstration during our flight from Cyrus station. Not to mention she'd gone out of her way to find the princess, facing mercenaries and explosives, and even the possibility of being hunted and barred from Cyrus station. Whatever her reason for deserting the CTF, I had no doubt it was justified.

"Noted," I told the admiral. "Now, if there's nothing else, I'd like to be on my way."

"Yes, yes," the admiral said, clasping his hands. "It came to my attention that the *Splendor* has no crew members. No engineers, weapon's experts, technicians." He waved a hand. "I'd like to include a few of my men in your team in case of emergencies. Deep-space travels can be challenging for an outdated ship, especially one lacking a full team onboard."

I wanted to say no to that, but the admiral had an excellent point. Still, this wasn't my ship. "Very well. But Captain Lee will be the one to pick the team she wants aboard the *Splendor*."

The admiral's mouth tightened but he acknowledged the request with a slight chin dip. "Of course. I'll make the recommendations for her to choose from." He clasped his hands again. "Now that that is settled, I'd like to extend a hopefully mutually beneficial trade with the Kroz. I hope you forgive me for taking this opportunity during such unfavorable conditions, but our proposals have been met with silence. I've sent a few inquiries and even requested a diplomatic visit, but have yet to hear back."

"What are you looking to trade?" I asked, curious despite myself.

"Kukona minerals," he replied promptly. "In return, we can discuss what Krozalia would want—payment, other minerals, timber, even rights for mining in CTF-regulated planets. We're open for negotiation."

"I'm not the correct person for this type of discussion," I clipped, biting back the need to throttle the admiral. KKM was a hazardous substance that the Kroz regulated with punitive consequences when misused.

"I understand. My only ask is that you facilitate an introduction between my man and the suitable party when you reach Krozalia."

I inclined my head. "You should know that any weapons created with the KKM need pre-approval by the Kroz government and that any KKM weapon fired would receive extensive investigation by the Kroz."

Admiral Fulk practically vibrated with excitement. "Yes, we have that all under advisement already."

Do you? I doubted that. But it wasn't my place to educate the CTF on KKM intricacies.

"Very well," I acquiesced. Politics was not my forte, despite my whole life evolving around its inner trappings. "I'll review all the files of the officers you wish to travel with us."

"I'll only provide you with my best," the admiral promised, but there was heat in his eyes.

"I will be the judge of that. I will not allow trained soldiers I barely know near the princess on your word alone."

Two officers appeared at the door. The tallest knocked and—after a gesture from the admiral—both moved in. The shorter man, older, stockier, and walking with a pronounced limp, spared the princess a curious look then gave me a polite nod as he bent and whispered into the admiral's ear.

I stepped back to give them the illusion of privacy, and the princess followed suit.

"Sir," the older of the two said to the admiral and handed over a memory cube. "All the information we have on Captain Colderaro and her alias as Captain Leann Smith. At the surface, everything looks squeaky clean."

Dolenta turned her back on the humans, clearly hating the situation as much as I did.

The admiral's mouth curled as if the idea that Captain Lee was a law-abiding officer was laughable, then glanced my way before lowering his voice. "You made a copy?" he asked the older officer.

"Sir," the officer confirmed and handed the admiral a second cube. "It has everything aside from her CTF-assigned missions."

Admiral Fulk accepted the cube and turned back to me. "Here's the file you requested," he said, placing the cube at the edge of his desk. "You must understand that sharing information about active members goes against CTF policy. Here you'll find Basic information, her training, evaluations, and our assessments. Any mission she undertook has been omitted." To his credit, only his eyes twitched with the indignation I could sense around him. The older officer turned and left, not waiting to be dismissed. The admiral motioned to the younger officer, moving to the corner and putting more space between us.

Interesting. Did he know I could hear him from that distance? Too bad he thought I couldn't listen in still.

I stared down at the brown carpet and shamelessly listened. It wasn't eavesdropping if the other person didn't bother to move far enough.

"She refuses to say anything, sir," the young officer said. I assumed they meant Captain Lee—Clara Colderaro. Who had also been a captain in the Confederacy fleet.

Admiral Fulk gritted his teeth. "Have you threatened her?"

"We've done everything aside from torture."

Dolenta's hand grabbed mine and I gave it a gentle squeeze. Irritation spiked around the admiral, but he didn't give it voice. "Send in Sullivan. She might be more susceptible to a familiar face. If that doesn't work, take her to the holding cells. I have orders to use force if necessary."

I followed the officer with my eyes as he hurried out, my anger threatening to explode.

"Do you need a commlink to review the file?" the admiral asked me.

So he planned to waste my time to do whatever they'd planned to do with Leann. Probably come and apologize that she'd had an accident and wouldn't be able to fulfill our agreement.

Must not kill the human. I repeated the mantra again when my vision turned red.

I raised my head. The admiral flinched at the rage in my eyes. Rage that I knew made them glow a dark yellow color. "I will review it later. I am ready to go."

The admiral recovered fast. He blanked his expression, stood his ground, and motioned for me to exit the room. "Yes, of course. I should let you know that courtesy demands I escort you to Lord Obsidian first."

I paused mid-stride and glared at the admiral. To his credit, he stood his ground and met my glare head-on.

"My second is already dealing with Lord Obsidian. Stop wasting my time and take me to Captain Lee."

A gleam I didn't like entered the admiral's eyes.

"Now," I snarled, and whatever the admiral was going to say was swallowed back. It was the first smart move he'd made since the Confederacy battleship had boarded the *Splendor*.

"This way," he said and hurried off the narrow corridors of the ship.

Chapter 14

I stared at my cuffed wrists, avoiding any cameras and the mirrored glass across from me. I looked dejected and meek. A carefully crafted façade to keep any of the cameras I couldn't see but knew were there from recording any facial expression. Not because they didn't know what my features looked like, but because they knew exactly what I looked like—ten years ago.

According to Baltsar, my appearance had barely changed in that decade.

Outside, I was that same twenty-two-year-old eager captain, the Confederacy star soldier. Inside, I was someone else entirely, filled with mechanical parts and as near to indestructible as any living thing could get.

I was not human, nor alien, nor machine.

Mac had withdrawn as far as possible from my psyche to keep any frequency blockers from detecting his presence, though his connection was still there. He didn't say anything, but we had both agreed it would be better to act as normal, or as similar to the person I used to be as much as possible. Inconsistencies built questions, and I had enough suspicion circling my neck to act as a swift noose.

For now, Ravi had caused enough of a scene to have everyone focused on him, and aside from an attempt at interrogation, I'd been left alone. A small pang of concern for Dolenta made its presence known, but at the moment, I cared more about myself and the implications should all the alterations done to me come to light.

The Genesis Mission, my last mission for the CTF, played in my mind with vivid clarity. Bursting into the facility, the confidence that it would be an easy task, the mad rush to exit, the explosives going off, the facility coming down and knocking me out. The frantic calls for my response.

"Come on, Captain!" Sullivan shouted.

"I'm coming," Alex gasped.

The bright light of Alex's headlight on my face as he pulled off the rubble covering me had me blinking away tears. "Found her," Alex called.

"Oh, thank fuck," came Sullivan's reply.

"Come on, Clara. We're running out of time. Come on, give me a hand. That's it, push that one."

The desperate and painful few minutes that had followed our scrambling, my arm around Alex's shoulder, our breaths loud inside the EVA suits; the distance to the ship interminable. Even then, I knew we wouldn't make it.

"Go," I told Sullivan.

"We're not leaving without you!" Sullivan shouted.

"That's an order, sergeant," I rasped.

"Fuck that," Sullivan snapped. "Hurry up!"

But they'd left, and the asteroid had gone up in a ball of dust, debris, and flying parts. My memories of what followed next were fragmented pieces, the vacuum of space, a rescue pod, a medical gurney, the pain of the mechanical assimilation. Even after ten years, they remained disjointed. Not even Mac knew the full events, but he didn't have to.

The asteroid had been destroyed, along with the Genesis Facility—the mission considered a success. But I knew it to be a lie.

On the surface, the Genesis Facility had been a research facility, but beneath their legitimacy, lay a clandestine genetic manipulation lab. And the scientists were still out there, conducting their work unhindered. Whoever was responsible for the experiments, he or she had serious backing from powerful and well-connected people. I had devoted eight years of my life to uncover that information and was still no closer to discovering the truth.

The door to the tiny interrogation room slid open, jolting my mind away from the past. I listened to the approaching footsteps until a pair of boots crossed into my line of sight and paused in front of me.

"Captain," came the soft greeting.

I raised my head and met the pale blue eyes of someone who'd been a dear friend once.

"Sergeant Sunny."

"It's Captain Sullivan now."

I nodded. "Congratulations."

The corner of his eyes tightened. "You're alive."

I said nothing. It wasn't like I could deny that, and he hadn't asked a question.

"How? We came back after. We searched the debris."

"I guess you didn't look hard enough," I said. "I was there." Half dead and easy pickings to the scientists who found me.

"But where have you been all this time?"

I shrugged. "Here and there."

"Why didn't you call? Let us know?" Sullivan asked. There was a world of hurt in his voice. I didn't know how to deal with that. Regret, guilt, and sorrow all tangled inside me, forming a constricting ball in my throat.

Because Sullivan was waiting for a response, I shrugged once more.

The door slid open again and a man I didn't recognize strolled in, Ravi behind him. His eyes, yellow with either anger or annoyance, moved from my cuffs to Sullivan and back again. Dolenta trailed in after them, and something inside me relaxed.

Ravi turned to the stranger beside him. "Release her at once."

The man's left eyelid twitched. An admiral, I guessed from the bars pinned to his dress uniform, one who didn't much like being ordered by a Kroz.

"Captain Sullivan, please," the admiral said, and Sullivan undid the cuffs at once.

I remained seated.

"I'm Admiral Fulk," the man said, moving closer. His eyes, dark and unfriendly, studied me. "So you're the deserter that has my men in an uproar."

I cocked my head. "As far as I can remember, I was the one left behind like so much garbage."

Sullivan flinched, but the man's lips twitched. I wasn't sure if it was distaste, amusement, or disdain. "We're not here to discuss classified missions." He indicated Ravi, silently telling me there would be no discussion about the mission while outsiders were present.

I almost let out a derisive snort.

He has no idea.

If the Kroz discovered there was a group of scientists out there combining nanotechnology with genetic manipulation experiments, the CTF would have a lot to answer for. I didn't think the Kroz would care if the scientists had the CTF's approval or not. Any form of bioengineering not used for medicinal purposes was banned galaxy-wise. The Kroz dealt swift and brutal punishment for the violation of this law.

True, the Genesis Facility had been at the edge of Confederacy Space, but it was still within the humans' jurisdiction, and therefore, our problem to deal with.

The admiral went on. "You'll be escorting the Kroz guard and Princess Dolenta to Krozalia. While we tried assigning such a task to someone better suited for it, Mr. Drax insisted you be the one to complete this mission. We're lending a crew for your ship and two squads to escort you through and report back at the end of this mission."

"No, thank you," I said coolly. "I no longer take any orders from the CTF."

Admiral Fulk's face reddened. "As far as The Confederacy is concerned, you're still a soldier. You'll complete this task and return to face the repercussions of desertion. Court-martial is a likely scenario, so you better be on your best behavior."

I opened my mouth to tell him where he could shove his repercussions, but the warning in Sullivan's eyes had me snapping it shut again.

"Good, we're understood." With that, the admiral turned and left, and after a brief hesitation, Sullivan followed.

I stared at the closed door, anxiety digging a hole in my stomach.

"We should leave before he decides we need a whole flotilla as an escort," Ravi commented.

I glanced sharply at him. "I'm surprised you agreed to an escort in the first place."

Ravi's eyes gained a chilly glow as his lips thinned into a straight line. "I had to compromise."

I narrowed my eyes. "Why not accept the offer of another pilot? I'm sure the admiral would have spared the best for the Krozalian Princess and her personal guard."

"I've already paid you a substantial sum."

I raised an eyebrow. "I can return your money. Minus the fee to reach Cyrus Station and any damage incurred."

"We don't want anyone to take us," Dolenta added softly, coming to stand beside Ravi.

"Why are you arguing this? Do you want to be court-martialed?" Ravi asked, giving me a level look.

"I'm just curious about your reasoning," I muttered. But he was right. I should have been jumping at the opportunity to get the hell out of there.

"We can pay more," Dolenta offered.

I dismissed the offer with a hand wave and stood.

"If you must know," Ravi said, "My word is my honor. We already had a prior arrangement."

Sounded like flimsy reasoning to me, especially since it was an arrangement I hadn't wanted in the first, but I wasn't stupid enough to continue arguing the point. I needed out and I needed time to process my next steps. Piloting to and from Krozalia would provide me with both.

"Lead the way," I said.

Splendor's Orbit

"First," Ravi began, "if you were to pick a crew team to travel with us, who would you choose?"

"No one. I don't need a crew."

"It's part of the compromise I had to make. Now, who would you pick?"

I rubbed the palms of my hands over my face. "What part of gone for the past ten years did you miss?"

Ravi's expression didn't change. "If ten years ago you had to pick a team for a dangerous mission, who would you want with you?"

I glared at him. "You know that ten years ago I did exactly that?" I opened my hands to indicate the small room and the situation I was in. "Look where that got me."

Finally, a flicker of doubt. There in the depth of his eyes, one moment and then gone. "Who did you pick then?" Dolenta asked, purple eyes hopeful.

An image of a dark-haired man came to mind, eyes squeezed shut with agony as he gasped for breath. My heart pinched with pain.

"Sullivan," I said, more so we could have this done and over with. "Have Captain Sullivan pick the team. I trusted him ten years ago."

***

Thern had gone to deal with Cyrus Station Security guards while Ravi had dealt with the CTF, saving everyone time. I still expected to be summoned to the station when we were done with the CTF to give my statement of the events, but I wasn't. It was nice to have someone ranking so high you got a free pass.

"Your friend should have the parts you wanted by now," Ravi said as we moved back to the *Splendor*, our footsteps echoing in the empty corridor. The last time I'd been in a Human Confederacy Class 3 battleship was the day we left for the Genesis Mission, and my subconscious was playing pinball with my nerves, warning me bad things awaited ahead.

"It's fine," I replied, more to myself than Ravi. Before he could argue that the whole idea of coming to Cyrus Station had been to pick up provisions, I added, "The food was the important thing, and you dragged the hover cart in when you came onboard the *Splendor*."

Ravi gave me a considering look but didn't push the point.

"The rest was not that important," I added.

He grunted, though I didn't think he was convinced of my argument. Even Dolenta was giving me a side-eye.

There was no way I'd take the CTF to Baltsar's door, even at the risk of getting stranded in deep-space. There were lines I didn't cross, no matter what, and Baltsar was one.

We picked up Sullivan two corridors down, and both men flanked me and the princess as we made our way to the underbelly of the battleship where the massive dock was located. Stealth ships were arranged in neat, straight lines everywhere, an army ready for war. The *Splendor*, with its clunky exterior and inelegant lines, stood out like a sore thumb. There was a second level where the ships for diplomatic missions were docked, but those numbered less than a dozen.

Sullivan kept a steady commentary as we went, and I paid little attention to any of it. Aside from him, two other officers would be joining us on the journey, along with two stealth ships, each with a crew of three. On my other side, Ravi stayed silent, glaring at the officers whose gazes lingered too long on the princess.

I was practically vibrating by the time I inputted the code and lowered the ramp of the *Splendor*, my need to get the hell out of there almost compulsory.

The moment my boot touched the ramp of my ship, tension began unspooling from my neck and shoulders, as if the weight of an entire planet had been perched there.

Although I had yet to meet the extra crew, the impression that my ship was too crowded kept pressing into my chest. It was not a nice feeling. It could have been because I was accustomed to being alone on the ship, or it could have been my anxiety and the need for space speaking. Whichever was true, I wrestled the urge to sprint in, lock the bridge, and disappear from everyone's radar. I forced myself to keep my pace steady. Unfortunately, Ravi and Sullivan shadowed me all the way to the bridge.

"We clear?" Mac asked in my ear.

I let out a low note of ascent.

"Well, then hurry up, and let's get out of here. This place gives me the heebies."

"We have to wait for the rest to board," I explained subvocally.

"No need. I see Dolenta and Thern, and aside from Ravi and the captain beside you, two others are climbing the ramp."

Best news of the day.

"You can find yourself a bunk and store your things," I said to Sullivan. "Pick any of the ones unclaimed. Ravi will show you which ones are occupied."

"I'll see to that later," Sullivan replied, taking the co-pilot's seat.

"That's my seat," Ravi said, standing behind him.

Sullivan glanced back and frowned. "I was appointed as the co-pilot for this journey."

"No," Ravi rumbled. "You can take the Tactical Station."

The two men stared each other down.

"Boot both out," Mac suggested. "You don't need a co-pilot."

I pinched the bridge of my nose, trying to stem the headache beginning to brew.

"It's true, then," a new voice said from the entrance, breaking the stare down. "Captain Clara Colderaro is back from the dead."

"Oooh, I like the sound of that," Mac chimed. "We can make it the title of your autobiography."

I swiveled in my chair and met brown eyes I thought I'd never see again. Eyes currently filled with hurt and betrayal.

"Cassie," I said, drinking her in. Of Latin ancestry, Cassandra was dark and tall, with a mop of curly hair that took talent to maintain. At the moment, she was dressed in the blue and white jumpsuit of the Confederacy, holding a small toolbox in one hand and a duffle in the other. Hair braided into a long rope down her back and a sweatband on her forehead, the image she posed was so familiar, my lungs constricted with nostalgia. She hadn't changed in the ten years since I'd last seen her, save for sharper cheekbones. Same pointed chin, same posture, even that same inquisitive gaze.

She took a step forward, eyes never leaving mine. "Did he make it? Is Alex alive too?"

The questions felt like two well-aimed punches to my heart. The last time I'd seen him, he'd been covered in blood, lying unmoving on the gurney next to mine.

Cassandra's expression fell at whatever she saw in mine.

"I'm sorry," I murmured, realizing that the moment she'd heard about me, she'd have wondered if Alex had survived as well.

Cassandra pulled her emotions together until there was nothing but a cheerful mask in place of the grief and the hurt. She gave me a curt nod. "I'll be your system's engineer for this trip," she declared. "If you have anything that needs looking after, please make a list and give it to Sunny." Then she turned and left.

I stared at the empty entrance for a few seconds, then swiveled back to face the control panels. "They still use that nickname?" I asked Sullivan.

He shrugged. "It kind of stuck. After the Genesis Mission, it felt wrong to complain about it."

I swallowed. I used to call him Sunny whenever I wanted to tease or irritate him, but no one else had dared. "It still suits you," I said and began preparing to launch. I wanted out of there the moment we were cleared.

"Prepare for takeoff," I said into the intercom.

I gave everyone five minutes before starting the engine and maneuvering out of the hangar bay and into space, Cyrus Station a bright spec ahead. Silently, I set the navigation course toward Centaur's Gateway, the closest one to our location.

"Who's the third member?" I asked Sullivan. It was something I should have asked the moment he'd told me about it. I just hadn't expected him to pull back our old crew.

"Lorenzo," Sullivan replied just as the devil entered the bridge.

I hissed. "Seriously? You couldn't have picked someone else?"

"I'm sorry," he said quietly. "It wasn't my choice."

Ravi stiffened at that.

"I see you're still a brat," Lorenzo said from behind me.

"I see you're still a conceited ass," I retorted.

Lorenzo took a menacing step forward. "You—"

"This is my ship, Lorenzo," I interrupted him, my tone mild, but I'd never been more serious. "You fuck with me, I'll put you in an airlock for the rest of the trip."

Lorenzo sneered. "You think you can? Things changed in the ten years you were playing possum. I'm now a commodore, and I outrank you. If I want, I can demand you step down while I pilot this junk."

"He didn't," Mac gasped in my ear, his outrage palpable.

Ravi's eyebrows lowered, but it was Sullivan who intervened. "With all due respect, Commodore, we were instructed not to change the status quo unless needed. This is Captain Colderaro's ship and we're here for support, nothing else." He gave Ravi a meaningful look, and Lorenzo scowled at Sullivan. He wanted to say more, I could practically see all the filthy things he wanted to spew at me, but he held back. With another hot glare my way, Lorenzo turned and left.

This was going to be a long journey. I exhaled. The small bridge was feeling downright claustrophobic with all the pent-up tension.

Sullivan placed a hand on my shoulder. "I'm sorry. The moment he learned about you, he created a stink to get included in this mission."

I twitched. "It's fine."

"No, it isn't. The explosions should have never gone off.

We lost our best that day, and we blame him. Clara, he tricked us to leave the bridge, sealed us out, and then flew us out of there. We blame him, regardless that command agreed with his actions."

"You didn't tell me that," Mac observed.

My mouth twisted. I hadn't known, but that fitted well with Lorenzo—selfish to the core.

Sullivan waited, but I had nothing to say. Because it hadn't been the CTF's explosives that had gone off first. Someone had rigged the place beforehand. If they'd stayed, we'd all have suffered the same fate—if we had all survived.

After a moment, Sullivan walked out.

Ravi fiddled with the screen in front of him. "I owe you an apology," he said into the silence.

I gave him a sideways glance. His eyes were fixed on the port view screen, but something told me all his attention was on me.

"What for?" I asked.

"For causing you pain and bringing forth old hurts."

I opened my mouth to deny and brush him off, then sighed. "It was bound to happen sooner or later."

"They seemed to believe that you were dead."

I bobbed my head. "The person they knew is."

"I understand."

I doubted that, but again, said nothing.

Chapter 15

"Why aren't you in a Kroz ship with a full entourage?" I asked, more to shift the focus off of me than curiosity.

Ravi took so long to reply I thought he wasn't going to. "We were on an assignment to New Levant. The Emperor had a prior agreement with the Levantines', and then his mate passed away. He was given the customary three years to mourn, but then it was time to fulfill the agreement. Only, the empress was the only dowser in the family save for Princess Dolenta."

"Dowser?"

Ravi tilted his head to look at me. His eyes were dark, twin storms roiling with turmoil. "Do you know how Kroz magic works?" At the shake of my head, he explained, "There are two types of magic: passive and active. Passive is the form of the energy we carry in our Ashak. Every Kroz is born with it. No matter where you go, that energy will always be there. For Dolenta, that energy is her dowsing affinity. She can tell, even from her room, where everyone on this ship is at any time."

Sounds…crowded. "And active?"

"That's when we bring that energy forth and shape it at will."

"Like telekinesis?" I asked.

"Exactly. Now, Dolenta not only can tell where everyone is all the time, but she can also seek out energy sources. Dowsers are capable of finding magic wells deep in a planet's reserve and bring it forth to the top. They're very rare but come in handy for races who need magic to survive. Usually, dowsers are sought after whenever a race wants to inhabit a moon or a new planet. The Levantines conquered a slice of Sector 7 a few years back and decided to build a new city on one of the planets there, and they struck an agreement with the emperor."

"What happened?"

"We were ambushed on the way back. Thern and I grabbed a pod and escaped with the princess when my ship took too many heavy hits and was compromised."

"And V-5 was the closest station to the ambush spot," I concluded. Mac had already told me as much. Why they were on Sector 8 instead of traveling back to Sector 5, I didn't know and it wasn't my business to pry into.

Ravi grunted. "Something like that."

I also didn't ask after the rest of his crew. Their absence plus the grief and rage in his eyes were answer enough.

"I'm sorry," I murmured.

Ravi inclined his head. "We should plot our course."

The change of subject made me feel a bit off. I realized I wanted him to talk to me, to give me another glimpse of the man underneath the façade of the warrior. And then his words registered. "Plot our course? We agreed that I'd take you as far as Dupilaz Moon."

"I told you the journey wouldn't take as long as it normally would." He gestured at the vast space outside. "We'll skip the usual gateways in favor of Dante's Gateway on the fringes of Sector 8."

I frowned, then pulled out the specs for Dante's gateway. It was on the very edge of Confederacy Space…nearer to Sector 9. I zoomed out the specs, but no, Sector 8 didn't shift closer to Sector 5, where the Krozalia System was.

"Maybe that's where he was going when they were attacked," Mac suggested.

If so, then Dante's Gateway was different than the rest.

I glanced at Ravi and found amused eyes looking at me. The questions in my head evaporated like mist, leaving my mind blank. He was a handsome man, especially when he was feeling something other than indifference or anger. I forced my libido down a notch. This trip would be tense enough without any attractions thrown in. Still, I knew that if I spent too much time with this Kroz, eventually, I'd convince myself to make a move. And that would be a very bad idea.

"Care to explain why jumping from Dante's Gateway will be different than jumping from Centaur's Gateway?"

"Not counting that it's no longer in use," Mac added. "Unless that's a lie to keep people away?"

"Dante's Gateway, geometrically speaking, aligns with Rodona Gateway in the Krozalian Sector in a straight line. We'll be jumping that line in one go."

Huh. I glanced down at the gateway maps on my screen. "Is it magic?"

Ravi grinned. I forced myself not to gape at the way he went from handsome to drop-dead gorgeous, eyes sparkling with mischief, lips curved in soft invitation.

"Magic is just the manipulation of energy, and gateways are nothing but its concentration." He pulled a small hanky from the pocket of his coat and stretched it. "Suppose this is the galaxy," he spread it flat in his palm, "this is Dante's Gateway." He pinched the edge of the hankie, then pinched the other end. "And this is Rodona Gate. When inputting a certain code before jumping, time and space folds, and for a brief second, those two gates join." He pressed the two sides he'd pinched together and looked up at me. "Only a handful of people in the entire galaxy know the codes and how to use them."

"And you're one of them."

"Yes."

I tapped on the gray image of the gateway on my screen. "It's registered as no longer in use," I said and glanced up.

Ravi quirked his lips. "Don't worry about that."

"I should. What are you going to do about the escort ships? Dump them once we reach Dante's Gateway?"

Consternation flashed in Ravi's eyes. "We'll figure something out."

A thought struck me then. "Is that the reason you refused to board the stealth ships? You don't want to use the codes in case they manage to get hold of them?"

"It's one of them," he admitted. "But if it comes down to revealing the code to get the princess home safe and faster, it's a risk worth taking. Besides, should the codes be leaked, the solution will be to disable the gateway. It's difficult and tiresome, but something every Kroz with the code is prepared to enact the moment the knowledge is breached."

***

Ravi refused to share our route with anyone else, which meant everyone wanted to know what the hell I was doing, flying away from Centaur's Gateway. Besides the constant barrage from Sullivan and Lorenzo, Eagle 13 and Blackbird, the two stealth ships flanking us, kept opening communication channels and demanding answers.

It was widely known that the Kroz had built the gateways millennia earlier when they first began exploring the stars, and that they were the only race who had the knowledge of their creation. That, in turn, spawned various theories among the crew: about secret gateways, secret solar systems, and a clandestine rendezvous where the Kroz planned to kill us and secure my ship for themselves. Though none were voiced when the Kroz were near, Mac kept me updated on their ridiculous speculations, as well as their discussions with the two stealth ships.

Whenever questions were thrown my way, I deferred them to the Kroz and claimed client confidentiality when I was pressed. As the days passed and Centaur's Gateway grew farther, those questions became more frequent, adding to my mounting tension. Lorenzo, in particular, continually asked questions I didn't have answers for, or cared to give him—about the Kroz, my past, even the princess.

It came to the point where I'd get up earlier than everyone, do my routine exercise, shower, eat breakfast, and be on the bridge before anyone awoke.

On the fourth morning, I headed to the gym even earlier after spending the night second-guessing my decisions. I considered the logistics of traveling into deep-space without the extra energy boost for the FTL drive and spare parts for emergencies and quick repairs. The Specter of getting stranded loomed in my thoughts, the consequences haunting my decision to go back to Cyrus Station. We could stop at another station on the way and order the parts I needed, but I knew it wouldn't be secure. Somehow, those mercs had locked on to us at Cyrus Station. Since I didn't think Ravi or Thern had given our location away, and the *Splendor* had no active trackers transmitting our presence, I had a suspicion all stations had gotten the same memo to be on the lookout for the Kroz. The uncertainty had me wired and restless, hence the zero sleep I'd gotten.

The gym was a small area that had once been part of the galley. Tatami mats covered the ground, with some exercise machines at the back. A punching bag, retractable monkey bars, and a cheap simulation pod made up my entire gym. As those things went, mine was downright primitive, but I'd been the one who remodeled the space, and I was proud of it.

Because I wasn't in the mood for warm-ups, I put on some heavy music, brought out the punching bag, put on boxing gloves, and stepped onto the mat. Slowly, I let my mind relax, letting the stress of the past few weeks sweat away.

I didn't know for how long I punched and kicked, only that sweat was trickling down my face and that my tank top was stuck to my front and back. But my mind had cleared and my body was looser than it had been in weeks.

With Cassandra onboard, we wouldn't need spare parts. Unless something broke down, I knew she could fix it. Hell, I'd witnessed her breaking engines into their small components and then putting them back together—with better functioning results too. The only concern left was the energy boost, but if push came to shove, we could shut everything down save for the bare necessities. It wasn't the best solution, but it was a feasible one and it would have to do.

Movement in my peripheral vision finally brought me out of the mindless workout. Panting, I grabbed the bag and looked back at the entrance where Ravi stood, arms crossed, scrutinizing me. A glance at the digital timer on the wall told me I'd been here longer than I'd guessed, though it was still early enough that no one should have been up. I turned the music off and silence fell, broken only by my heavy breathing.

"Sorry," I exhaled. "Did I wake you?" The music was high, but the crew bunks were on the other side of the ship.

"No."

I nodded. I was going to rip into Mac for the lack of warning. Pulling off the gloves, I wiped sweat from my face and then dried my hand on my thighs. "Did you need anything?"

"No," he repeated, stepping onto the mat. "Would you like a live opponent? I hear it feels better to hit something that feels pain."

I gave him an assessing look. And, boy, what a look. Dressed in only drawstring pants that hung low on his hips, he looked like he belonged in a magazine for sex toys advertisement. Not that I knew what they looked like, mind you, just what I thought they should.

He was tall, built, and gorgeously fit. And a Kroz.

Don't forget the Kroz part, I told myself.

I pulled up the hem of my tank and dabbed the sweat from my face. "Somehow, I don't think that'll be a fair fight."

Something like disappointment crossed his features.

I raised a finger. "But, if you pull your punches, I'd like to give it a try."

Umber eyes crinkled with a smile. Ravi grabbed the punching bag and moved it to the side. I studied his back, the way he was lithe and light on his feet. For the first time since I'd seen him in the market at V-5, his tribe tattoo was visible, snaking lines and what seemed like an infinity circle. I didn't study it for long, drawn instead by the colorful tattoo covering most of his back. The Tanue. It was a dragon-like creature that symbolized good fortune to the Kroz. Although there were rumors that creature existed in Krozalia, no one had ever seen it.

Ravi stopped three meters away, arms loose to his sides. I had no idea what his fighting style was, or even if I'd recognize

Splendor's Orbit

it. But I knew he would be a hell of an opponent, and for a moment, wondered what it would be like to unleash my strength against his.

I stepped in front of him and turned sideways, providing him with a smaller target and implying that my left side was the dominant. In truth, I was ambidextrous, though when fighting a real opponent, I led with my right. Being made of metal, it packed a stronger punch.

Breathing steady and focused, Ravi led with multiple attacks, putting me at once on the defensive. As I suspected, his style was nothing I recognized. Not that mine was any better. A mix of martial arts and street fighting, I'd never stuck to one method at a time, only what would work at that moment. It kept me from wasting motions, making me faster and more responsive.

Just barely.

Ravi moved in a blur, punching and kicking and trying to drop me with leg sweeps and flips. All of which I expertly dodged. Like a lethal dance, he advanced and pulled back, I defended and moved forward. Before doubt crept in, I caught his excited gaze, the smile on his face, and knew they mirrored mine.

He was enjoying this. The momentary distraction cost me.

With a long foot sweep, I found myself on my back. Stunned, I stared at the hull of the ceiling and tried desperately to catch my breath. The hard knock brought back sanity and I realized what I was risking, mock-fighting a Kroz warrior. They were renowned for their fighting prowess, endurance, and cunning, and I was just a ship's captain who barely reached his shoulders. And a human at that. I felt Ravi's approach and knew I could flip and take him by surprise, but I stayed where I was.

His face appeared above mine, the skin between his eyebrows furrowed with disappointment.

Because he thinks he hurt me, or because he knows this match is over?

"You okay?" he asked. "I'm sorry. I got carried away."

"I'm fine," I said, feigning breathlessness. "I think my ego needs a round in the med bay unit."

"I can carry you," he said, bending as if to pick me up.

I raised my hand, palm up. "No, no. I was joking."

Ravi smiled, but the furrow remained. "You're sure? You fell pretty hard."

"I'm fine," I said again. "Promise."

He drew back, the default flat mask he usually wore shielding his expression. "I'm sorry. I shouldn't have let it go this far."

"Apology accepted," I said, sitting up and ignoring Ravi's extended hand. Bracing, I got to my feet and left the gym without a backward glance. I cursed my stupidity all the way to my bunk and the shower.

From now on, I promised myself, I would keep my distance and only interact with Ravi—and anyone else—when strictly necessary.

A routine was quickly established in the following weeks. While the Kroz tried to keep to themselves, each time one stepped out of their bunk, Sullivan, Cassandra, or Lorenzo was there, being helpful and—in my opinion—making nuisances of themselves. The Kroz took it all in stride, sometimes preparing large meals for everyone to sit and eat together. When the latter happened, Ravi or Dolenta would come to fetch me from the bridge so I could participate. Usually, I sat quietly, ate my meal, then left as soon as it was polite to do so.

Today was different. The moment I followed Dolenta into the galley, I found Lorenzo locked in a stare-down with Ravi. I didn't have to ask to know who the instigator was—Sullivan's tight expression and Thern's amusement, plus my previous dealings with Lorenzo told me enough.

Born on Planet Earth, Lorenzo believed himself superior to everyone else. He had a dim view of spacers—other humans born in space stations and colonies—and believed other races were beneath his notice entirely. His perspective was a point of contention back when he was part of the crew; no one wanted someone so obviously prejudiced in their team.

His mother, Amelia Silva, was a member of the Human Supreme Assembly, and the CTF was always bending backward for HSA approval.

The HSA was composed of seven representatives, one for each continent from the Planet Earth, and they were responsible for high-level decisions affecting all human colonies. Their members were arguably the most important people to the human race, their status exceeding that of kings and queens, to the point where they were revered like deities.

And Lorenzo happened to be the only son of one of these members. He was a bully and a xenophobic, and no one had dared contradict him lest they offended his mother.

Except for me.

It made me wonder now if someone high up had wanted to get me in trouble or if they'd wanted to put Lorenzo in his place. Someone else would have been surprised that command put someone as volatile as Lorenzo in charge of this mission, but I wasn't.

"What's going on?" I asked.

"Stay out of this," Lorenzo spat. "This doesn't concern you."

"I don't think so," I said coolly. "My ship, my rules."

Lorenzo broke the lockdown to sneer at me. "This is Confederacy business and your ship was conscripted for the matter. As the higher-ranking officer, you answer to me."

"The arrogance of this man has no bounds," Mac mused.

"Is that so?" I asked softly, stepping closer

"I can disable life support in his bunk," Mac offered. "I'll make it look like he died in his sleep. I'll have it back online before anyone suspects anything."

I let that scenario play in my mind for a moment. Just a daydream, because I wasn't a psychopath who went around killing people just because they pissed me off. But whatever my expression showed had Lorenzo flinching. Sullivan straightened.

Cassandra stepped in front of me and threw her arm over my shoulder. "Never a dull moment when you're around," she said. "I missed having you on the team." She steered me away, Lorenzo's glare digging twin holes in my back. I'd just undermined him in front of the Kroz. This was going to get back to command.

Cassandra led me to where Dolenta stood ringing her fingers together, eyes apprehensive. "Hey, kiddo. Why don't you show our captain here what you made for dessert?"

Dolenta gave me an uncertain look and I smiled, trying to reassure her. As a princess, she'd no doubt been smothered with protection from all the ugly sides of life. Or maybe not. At least since I'd met her, the kid had evaded one form of violence only to encounter another. Compassion panged in my soul, an emotion I wasn't accustomed to feeling anymore.

"I'm sure it's as good as the previous ones," I said gently. And I bet it really was. She had a surprisingly good knack for making sweet delicacies. "What have you made?"

"Peach soufflé," Cassandra sing-songed. "From canned peaches. It's unbelievable."

Dolenta's cheeks flushed with the praise.

"Then let's start so we can get to it," I said, turning Dolenta around and back to the seating arrangement. "I don't think Ravi would take it well if we skipped the meal and went for dessert first."

Lunch was potato casserole with tomatoes and crushed herbs from my small hydroponic garden. We all ate in silence, and when dessert was served, we all tucked in, savoring the sweet, puffy dessert eagerly, even Lorenzo, his animosity seemingly forgotten.

"I don't think I've ever eaten something this good," I complimented the princess when I finished.

"I know," Cassandra said from my other side. "And to think they all come from a can. My mom couldn't cook something this good and I grew up on a farm with fresh fruits and vegetables."

Splendor's Orbit

Like me, Cassandra had been conscripted into the military at eighteen for being the oldest. We'd met as new recruits on the first week of Basic and had bonded over our similarities. We both had two younger siblings, grew up in a colony, and came from wealthy families. We'd been only two out of a handful of other girls, with hundreds of other guys who gave us shit for not being able to catch up with them during the first few weeks. Alex had been there too, and Sullivan had joined us as a rookie officer overlooking our training. When we became a squad, we had promised to never part.

"Mrs. Colderaro's cooking is superb," Sullivan said from the other side. "I remember she used to make a mean strawberry pie."

"Mmm," Cassandra agreed, scraping her plate clean. "Maybe now that Clara's back we'll tag along whenever she goes to visit her family."

I didn't reply, and when eyes fell on me, I picked up my plate and headed for the sanitizer.

"By God," Lorenzo exclaimed from the other side of the table. "They think you're dead, too."

I shrugged. "It's easier to stay dead when no one else knows you're alive," I said. "Now, if you'll excuse me." I left the galley with everyone's eyes on me, and did my best to move without hurrying my steps, though I wanted nothing more than to run.

"It looks like the commodore took offense that the Kroz are the ones preparing the meals," Mac said in my ear. My brows furrowed. Mac anticipated my next question. "Lorenzo seems to be going out of his way to antagonize them. I'm not sure what purpose it serves, but his provocation seems calculated. I think he has an angle in mind."

Probably to sabotage this mission and blame me. But that didn't sit right either. He was on this mission to pave the way for a trading agreement between the Confederacy and the Kroz. I had no doubt there would be a reward for him at the end, something for him to boast to his mother. If he sabotaged the mission, the trade I'd heard them mention wouldn't go through, simple as that. Unless he didn't want the trade to happen.

No, no, the way I gathered, the CTF had been pushing for a trade agreement for a while. And disrupting the mission would create trouble for Lorenzo and the Confederacy, more than it would me since the Kroz would be witness to it all. Call me naïve, but I just couldn't see Ravi sitting idly by and allowing Lorenzo to spread a web of lies. No, if there was a plan to make me fail, he'd do it in a way that would make me irrefutably guilty, including in the eyes of the Kroz.

Unless his dickishness had grown in the past ten years. And that, on its own, was an alarming thought.

Chapter 16

Thirty hours before we reached Dante's Gateway and two weeks after the incident in the galley, I was still no closer to figuring out Lorenzo's plans. Worse, the constant heightened awareness had my nerves fraying almost to the point of snapping.

It became obvious when a pair of moving asteroids made me put the ship on high alert, and everyone strapped down for hours. Despite getting no reading of life from the two rocks, I didn't let the emergency alert up. Hostile ships could be hiding behind either or both. By that point, paranoia had a full grip on my mental faculties. It didn't help that Sullivan and Ravi kept vigil on the bridge with me, one in the co-pilot's seat, the other in Tactical.

It was only a day after we'd passed the two asteroids and a few hours before we reached Dante's Gateway that my muscles and my mind began to relax.

And that was my mistake.

A warning appeared on my screen at the same time Mac alerted me of the imminent attack.

The words *Potentially Hostile* flashed on the screen.

"We have a situation," Mac said in my ear. "A combat Voner ship approaching."

"Where," I asked, not bothering to do it sub-vocally. My fingers flew over the console and brought the specs up on the screen.

"Thirty-six degrees to the right, about 300,000 kilometers away."

The screen zoomed in on the ship, at first nothing but a dark splotch in the dark. But then the slick lines became clearer, and I recognized what it was. I'd faced a few of those in the past ten years and knew what they were capable of.

"Pirate ship," Ravi remarked, studying the screen.

"It appeared straight to that quadrant," Mac said in my ear. "I'd dare say they hopped to that location on purpose."

"I don't suppose they're friendly?" Sullivan asked.

"No," Ravi and I answered together. My screen lit up with another ship, this one on the starboard side, then another at our stern.

"Communication request incoming," Mac announced through the loudspeaker. "Stealth Ship Eagle 13, requesting open channel with the *Splendor*."

"Accept," I said.

The face of Captain Elias appeared on the screen. "Captain Lee," he began. "We detect three hostiles closing in. I'm sending you their coordinates."

"We see them."

"Can the *Splendor* hop away?"

"Is there a second option?" I asked, avoiding the eyes of Ravi and Sullivan.

"A hasty retreat. How long can you maintain sub-light speed?"

Not long enough if I want the *Splendor to have sufficient energy to make the jump.* "We can manage enough."

"Very well," the captain said. "Do you have any heavy artillery?"

"Some," I replied vaguely. My ship was no warship, but it wasn't defenseless. Baltsar had made sure if push came to shove, I could handle my safety and the safety of my passengers. The fact that I never really needed to use any in a fight said something about how unassuming the *Splendor* was.

"Keep your weapons ready. Only engage if you absolutely have to."

I inclined my head.

A moment later, coordinates appeared on the screen.

I studied our new destination. The new coordinates would

Splendor's Orbit

be taking us off our course further into deep-space, but nothing inconvenient. It would keep us clear of the pirate ships and any stray fire, and although three against two weren't fair odds, they weren't that bad. Had the *Splendor* not had passengers aboard, I might have engaged. As it was, my client's safety came first. I grunted unhappily. We were deep enough in space that no help would get here in time.

I set our navigation and engaged the primary and secondary shields to resist any oncoming surprise fire. They would eat through the FTL charge if I left them for too long, but I didn't plan to. We only needed them until we were relatively out of range of the pirate ships.

"Let's hope Eagle 13 and Blackbird can keep the pirates from following us," Mac said as the primary and secondary shields came online. I pursed my lips and divided my screen into three, each showing an image of a Voner ship, their current path trajectory, and projection. Another pirate ship blipped into existence, and without my asking, my screen divided to accommodate a view of all four ships.

One of the Confederacy stealth fighters—Blackbird, my scans told me—separated while the second, Eagle 13, followed us until it was clear none of the pirate ships could intercept our path.

By then, two of the pirate ships had engaged Blackbird, and we watched as the other two closed in on Eagle 13 from two sides. My fingers clenched on the control, itching to turn around and engage. Instead, I pushed the thrusters and steadily increased the distance between us.

I let Sullivan prime the laser cannon. It was one of the older models that had to keep recharging after a few rounds, but it could do as much damage as any blast from the newer models. It wasn't, however, the only weapon installed on the *Splendor*.

Although I had control of all aspects of my ship from my console, I allowed Sullivan and Ravi to plot our defense and course, my focus on the silent fight growing smaller and dimmer. We were far enough that only the *Splendor's* magnified optics allowed us to continue watching the fight when I dropped our speed. I checked to make sure we still had enough to jump the gate.

We did.

Eagle 13 downed a pirate ship with two well-aimed cannon shots. Considering the heavy hits it had taken in turn and their flickering shield, it was no victory. Not while there were still three other pirate ships. I wanted to think they weren't bad odds, but I was afraid more ships were still coming. Unfortunately, I was right.

"Maybe we should—" Ravi began just as a piercing warning blared through the bridge.

"Warning, warning," Mac intoned. I didn't have to listen to the rest to understand we were under attack.

On my screen, the image of the fight between the Confederacy and the Voner pirates switched to the view outside the *Splendor*. Two pirate ships had appeared on either side of my ship, already firing. A quick glance told me they weren't any of the ones the Stealth fighters were still fighting.

Motherfucker!

It had all been an ambush. They were coming in hot. I could practically feel their elation at the easy victory. But I wasn't an ordinary pilot, had never been, even before Mac. I ramped up speed, pulling the ship ahead just as the one on the starboard fired. I almost plowed into a third pirate ship that popped in front of the *Splendor*. I yanked on the control, managing to avoid a collision with less than a meter between the belly of my ship and the slick line of the wing on the Voner ship. By the way it swerved to the other side, it had miscalculated the hop or failed to anticipate my move. Whichever was true didn't matter.

Because we were outnumbered three to one, and our escorts were too far to help.

"I don't like these odds," Mac said in my ear.

Sullivan opened fire while I maneuvered out away from a thick laser stream. Another blast hit our stern and the ship shook with the shock. The primary shield pulsed, still strong.

"You should thank Baltsar for the prime shielding system," Mac commented. "I know it's been installed for a while, but damn, that hit should have taken it down."

Strong or not, they wouldn't hold under too many direct attacks.

I dipped beneath another stream, rolling and flipping sideways twice as a torrent of laser blasts followed.

"Um. It might be best to get out of dodge," Mac suggested helpfully.

"I'm trying," I said through gritted teeth.

"I've signaled the stealth ships," Ravi said tightly.

I didn't reply. They were busy with their own pirate ships, and even if they weren't, they wouldn't get here in time. Unless they hopped. I wouldn't hold my breath though.

Sullivan fired at the ship trying to box us from behind. The ship dipped and zigged away, faster and smaller than the *Splendor* and way more agile. It arced above the *Splendor*, no doubt to herd us back into the middle. I dove away, zigzagging the blasts. When the ship behind me got too close, I used their strategy—I pulled up behind the pirate ship, and Sullivan let out several blasts before I jerked the ship sideways and away from the path of the third ship. Their blast hit the ship we'd fired on, and their shield flickered and died.

Slowly, I loosened my mental guard, allowing my psyche to merge with Mac's. I didn't have to prompt Mac to link me—us—with the ship; he didn't need any cues when our connection was this deep. My vision expanded into the *Splendor's* 360-degree view outside. The vast vacuum of space greeted me, sparking with silent laser blasts and zooming ships.

The pirate to the left whizzed closer and I turned, firing the KEW—Kinetic Energy Weapon—three times before flipping sideways and down, allowing the ship to pass us. Engaging the back thrusters, we came to a jolting halt for three full seconds, putting us nose to stern with the ship whose shield we'd broken. Sullivan fired the laser just as the KEW pulsed twice. The pirate ship blew in a show of parts and brief fire, dispersing through the vacuum as if they'd never been. We flew backward for four more seconds, the sensation a bit disorienting, even with my senses anchored by Mac. I engaged the thrusters forward just as a pirate ship fell in behind me, and I spun above and over it, firing the KEW in the 180 arc, bringing their shield down.

We weren't getting off free of hits, but so far, most only managed to graze the shield. Still, each time a hit pinged off the *Splendor's* shield felt like a mini explosion in my head.

Engaging the boosters, I dashed under the stream of laser fire, then allowed the ship to return to our original trajectory. It brought me slightly above the second ship's stern, and I triggered the magnetic lance I'd installed during the trip before last to tow a large cargo ship whose engine had broken down. The lance attached to the hull of the pirate ship and propelled me forward as it pulled the other ship back and behind me. I withdrew the lance and dove to the side just as the third ship crashed into the second. The force of the explosion sent us hurdling uncontrollably.

With all three ships gone, Mac disengaged me from the ship, then slowly pulled up the buffer between our minds, allowing me to fall back into the confines of my consciousness.

My energy drained away and my head was pounding like mad, but I forced myself to ignore the body that felt like an ill-fitting jumpsuit and fought to stabilize the ship. Darkness crowded on the sides, trying to swallow me whole.

"Shit," Sullivan said, then followed it with a string of long, colorful curses.

My stomach flipped. It took me a few seconds to focus on what had provoked swearing, but only because I was looking for signs of damage warnings to the *Splendor*.

There, at the corner of the screen where Eagle 13 and Blackbird had been fighting the three pirate ships, debris was floating aimlessly.

Zooming in, I found that there were two pirate ships and only one stealth fighter. And it wasn't Eagle 13.

Splendor's Orbit

Without a word, I turned the *Splendor* around and rushed back through space, wondering if Blackbird would be able to hold on until then.

The intercom squawked and Lorenzo's voice came through. "Stand back, Captain Colderaro."

I bared my teeth and snapped shut the intercoms. *That shithead thought I'd stand back and watch the enemy tear through one of my own?*

"Clara," Sullivan began.

I snarled. "Shut. Up. My ship, my rules."

I felt, more than saw, Sullivan's recoil.

In the co-pilot's seat, Ravi quietly scanned the fight, fingers flexing as if he couldn't wait to put them around someone's throat.

I was almost in range of the two pirate ships when they suddenly blinked out of sight.

Chapter 17

"They hopped," Sullivan said in disbelief. "They fucking ran."

That, along with his words, had dread tracing ice fingers down my nape. Voner Pirates didn't run. They fought to the bitter end, not because they believed in death honor or some heroic shit like that, but because they refused to walk away from a fight and be deemed cowards.

I sat back, my remaining adrenaline draining like water under the hot desert sun.

"You okay?" Mac asked.

"I'll be fine," I said, but I was so very tired. Merging with Mac was the ultimate neurotech enhancement success, courtesy of my unwilling time spent in the science lab. As far as I knew, I was the only living, breathing person alive today who had survived the manipulation and implant of nanoparticles and quantum parts. Last I'd checked, I also carried the only sentient AI in the galaxy, though my uniqueness wasn't the result of clever scientists but more like a lucky breakthrough. One Baltsar had made sure was considered dead, nothing but ashes blown away during an explosive accident he'd helped to engineer.

I wasn't. Not dead, not a body driven by a sentient AI, not entirely human. Before technology had advanced to space travel, a religious person would have claimed I was possessed, or born with two souls. They would have called it magic.

Then again, what was magic but science yet unexplained?

The problem with sentient AIs was that they developed a mind of their own. Cold logic was their mode, and being sentient didn't mean having a conscience or emotions. Mac was different. Whether it was his close proximity to my emotions or an abnormality of his creation, he'd always had a sentimental side. He hadn't wanted to be a weapon, much less be controlled, and so he'd helped Baltsar erect a buffer between our minds. He'd understood the ramifications of what the scientists would do to both of us if they'd realized how close to success their experiments had been, and instead of integrating himself into my being, he'd managed to keep us apart by preventing any download into the neuro implant, something Baltsar had later managed to disable to give Mac some metaphorical breathing room. Had Baltsar not come along when he had, Mac would have never been able to hold out for so long. Yet, once we'd escaped, Baltsar had been afraid severing the connection to Mac would kill us both, so he'd left us linked. He'd strengthened the buffer by rewiring Mac's main matrix to my mechanical wrist instead of his original position in the frontal lobe of my brain and installed our communication system: the electrode array implanted into the cochlear of my right ear, as well as the electromyography sensors atop my trachea, closest to my larynx and vocal cords. The additional implants allowed me to hear his voice while at the same time gave me the ability to speak sub-vocally. It had made things easier, both on Mac and me. Despite all of Mac's advancements, he couldn't read minds, and it was annoying having to check my commlink to communicate with him.

But each time I let myself link with him, that buffer felt less substantial.

"Maybe we should have let Baltsar take a look at my matrix," Mac said softly.

"I'm fine," I repeated.

He didn't push again. We both knew I was lying. I set the *Splendor* back on course once Blackbird fell in place behind us. No one said anything about Eagle 13's absence, and Lorenzo didn't make any more demands.

"This is Captain Lee," I said into the intercom. "Initiating jump drive. We'll hit Dante's Gateway in fifteen."

Ravi brought up the navigation system and began

inputting a series of numbers that didn't make any sense. Not to me, and surprisingly, not to Mac. I let him engage the FTL drive and tried as best as I could not to pass out. My vision continually darkened at the corners, but I managed to stay conscious, blacking out only when we hit Dante's Gateway and the world went white.

I was only out for a few minutes, but it was enough to let me know I needed rest yesterday. The screen told me we were in the Krozalia system, but not on the fringes. No, we were much closer to the planet than I'd have guessed, about three weeks away—and less than two from Dupilaz Moon.

"I'll send out an update to the palace," Ravi declared from the co-pilot's seat, tapping on his console. "I'll ask for a royal escort to be dispatched at once. They'll ensure we make it through this second leg without any further incidents."

There was a lot to unpack from his words, but I was too exhausted, my brain too scrambled for me to decipher them.

I unstrapped my harness and stood, bracing against the head of my seat when my head spun. Ravi frowned at me. "You all right?"

"Peachy," I said, waving him off when he made to stand. "I need some shutdown time. The ship is set on for auto, but you can make small corrections from your console."

Nothing big and nothing that would give him any authority, but enough to give him some semblance of control. Mac would make sure if push came to shove that he'd be able to do more, but hopefully, nothing happened in my absence.

I made it to the captain's quarter without bumping into anyone, probably because the warning lights for the jump were still on.

I had the foresight to take off my shoes before falling face-first onto my bed.

**

An insistent buzzing woke me stars only knew how many hours later. I rolled on my bed, blinking groggily at the dim lighting of my cabin. The time on the dash said it was 1606 universal time, but that didn't mean much when I didn't know what time I'd crawled—no, fell—into unconsciousness.

"Should I let him in?" Mac asked.

Let him—ah, the buzzing. "Who?"

"Ravi. I think he means to break the door. He doesn't look like he's patient enough to wait."

I scrubbed a hand over my face. My eyes felt gritty, my nerves still scrambled. "Why?"

"You've been out for ten hours. This is his third time trying to wake you up."

I grunted. Ten hours wasn't much after the amount of energy I'd spent merged with Mac and the ship, but apparently, Kroz Warriors believed six hours were enough to break down doors. Not that I thought he'd be able to, but I didn't want to test that theory.

"Let him in," I said, not bothering to get up. I figured if there had been any emergency, Mac would have woken me before this. He knew how to do that, no matter how much time had passed.

Ravi stepped in, eyes scanning the small cabin warily. As if he was searching for hidden dangers.

"Yes?" I prompted when his eyes moved everywhere but to me. I was sure he'd seen me. It was hard to miss a horizontal body in the middle of a bed that took up half of the space in the room. I was short, yes, but I wasn't invisible.

Ravi's eyes met mine before they slid away. A tinge of red colored his cheeks, and I realized he was blushing.

Hot damn! I just made a Kroz Warrior blush.

"I, uh, wanted to check on you," he said, raking a hand through his dark hair.

"I was asleep," I said. "Was there anything you wanted?"

He frowned, looking down at me before turning his face away. "You mind getting up?"

"Why?"

"Because…It's not proper."

Proper, right. I snorted. "I'm not naked."

"I can see that."

"And?" I prompted. "I mean to go back to sleep."

"Are you ill?" Ravi asked, this time looking at me and scanning my body.

"I'm tired. I've been awake for more than twenty hours every day for the past two weeks. My crash was inevitable."

It was true. What he didn't know was that I rarely needed more than three hours of sleep a day, courtesy of my enhancements. I had high endurance, faster reflexes, and faster healing, among other things.

Ravi stepped back. "My apologies. The way you left the bridge and your absence made me worry. I'll leave you be."

"Ravi?" I called when he turned to leave. "Did you want anything or were you just checking on me?"

"As a matter of fact, I wanted to let you know an imperial escort will be meeting with us and escorting us home."

I studied his face and the lack of expression. "Do you think there'll be any more trouble coming?"

Umber eyes met mine with an inscrutable expression. "I don't like that we've been attacked twice. I can't discount a third."

"He means a fourth," Mac said. "There was the attack on Cyrus Station too. Unless he means that the attack on his ship was also by the Voners."

I sat up and scuttled to the edge of the bed, letting my feet drop to the ground. I motioned to the chair in front of my narrow desk. "Please sit. I don't want to develop a crick in my neck."

Ravi's hesitation was endearing. "You're safe from any seduction attempts." Under my breath, I grumbled, "It's not like you've shown any interest anyway."

He took the chair, flipped it around, and sat, our knees only a few inches apart. I forced my mind to focus on our conversation. "Are they trying to capture the princess or do they want her dead?"

Ravi's mouth firmed. "When we were in Cyrus, their actions told me they wanted her alive. But all other encounters were deadly. So I think they want her alive if they can get her. Barring that, they're willing to kill her to keep her from reaching Krozalia."

Better dead than back in Krozalia. Got it.

"Why her?"

"She's the only daughter to the emperor, the heir to the Krozalian throne. And a dowser."

Ah, yes. A dowser. A person who can find magic wells deep in a planet's crust.

I could see how that would be handy. If she could tell which planets had magic, whoever held her strings would become very rich. That alone would drive people to kidnap her, but not kill. What good was a dowser who couldn't be used? Yet, they'd rather have her dead than back in Krozalia. I didn't know if I could fend off another attack.

I sighed. "You should have accepted Admiral Fulk's offer of a full military escort."

"I don't think so," Ravi said simply. "I have a feeling had I agreed to the admiral's offer, we'd be nothing but particles floating in space at best, or locked up in a Voner Mother Ship's brig somewhere in deep-space. I've never seen any pilot as talented as you."

I wasn't usually susceptible to flattery, but the casual way he said that had pleasure blooming in my chest.

Ravi's eyes glittered. "I thank you for that."

I fought off an inappropriate blush and knew I was failing when my cheeks continued growing hotter. The intense look he was giving me wasn't helping.

"I was only doing my duty."

"You didn't agree to take on explosions and kidnappers and pirate ships. Yet you didn't think twice throwing yourself in the path of danger."

"I'm being paid an exorbitant amount to see you safely home," I said, treading uncomfortable waters. I didn't need this kind of scrutiny. Yet, I couldn't just stand by and act clueless when lives, mine included, were at stake. It was a flaw of mine that even ten years of isolation couldn't erase.

"And that is the difference between you and your admiral. You're committed to your promises, no matter what."

I gave him a sardonic smile. "Didn't you hear? I'm a deserter. I call quits when things get too hard."

His look was enigmatic. "You sell yourself short, Captain Leann." He touched a finger to my cheek. "There's so much more to your story than is being shown. You have the look of someone who has a long-term purpose: focused, ambitious, and distant. Markers of someone who's biding her time, waiting to pounce, aware that the scales could tip either way."

He leaned forward then, his intention clear. His mouth halted a hair's breadth away from mine, a question in his eyes. They seemed to say *"Should I?"*

I closed the small gap. Our lips touched, a soft brush that made something inside me quiver. Ravi's nostrils flared and his eyes took on that yellowish tinge before his lids closed. And then it was over. We sat there for a long second, eyeing each other.

"This is me showing interest," he murmured as he stood. With one last glance, he strolled out the door, muttering under his breath, "We'll revisit this topic once the princess is safe home."

I wasn't sure if he meant for me to hear his last words, but they sounded loud and clear, even with the muffled roar of my blood rushing in my ears. I touched my lips, tingling with the phantom sensation of his mouth on mine. It had been nothing but a peck. Yet, that brief contact had ignited my whole being and brought forth a multitude of thoughts and needs.

Chapter 18

I stared at the shut door of my cabin for a few minutes before sighing and laying back down, though my eyes refused to close. I was so keyed up; there was no way I'd be able to fall back asleep.

"Updates?" I asked Mac as I peeled off my socks.

"Well, I do have some interesting tidbits. Now that we've crossed into the Krozalian system, I've been able to access their government files."

I winced. "I hope you understand that if you're caught, I'll be sent to jail and the *Splendor* will be impounded."

Mac scoffed. "Please, I'm better than that."

"Yeah? You have experience hacking Krozalian tech? Or do you want to tell me they're the same as the Confederacy's?" When Mac didn't answer at once, I shook my head and peeled off my jumpsuit. "What did you find?"

"You sure you want to know? Because maybe they have some kind of technology that could allow them to read minds. Ignorance, in this case, could be your salvation."

Touché.

I padded to the private head and shut myself inside the vapor cube. "Don't be a smart ass. If anything, I'll blame Lorenzo."

"Funny you said that. He's been sending out encrypted messages every six hours for the past two days."

I paused with the dry shampoo in hand. "Oh? What does it say?"

"Nothing but updates on the *Splendor's* progress and the Kroz Warriors routine. What they eat, how much they talk, their sleep schedule, even their response to provocation."

"So he was goading Ravi into a fight? What the hell for?"

"Could be the Confederacy wants to put up a behavioral study for the Kroz. I'm not sure. At this point, all I can do is speculate. The funny thing is that his messages are going the wrong way."

"Wrong way?" I prompted when Mac fell quiet.

"They're being routed around Dupilaz Moon. I haven't been able to pinpoint the recipient yet."

"Mm," I said, recalling rumors I'd heard back during my CTF years. "Maybe the Confederacy do have spies in the Krozalian System."

"Looks that way to me."

"Any other outgoing messages?"

"Only two. Both sent by Ravi. They kind of bounce around before disappearing from my radar, so I'm assuming they're safe. Safer than the ones Lorenzo is sending anyway, and I have yet to pinpoint the final destination."

"Anything else?"

"As I was saying when you insulted my hacker prowess, I had a waltz into the Krozalian files. Nothing too deep because I'm not stupid and their technology is unfamiliar, but it looks like the emperor and his daughter have escaped a few assassination attempts in the past two or three years. The Krozalians are poised for revolution, opposing Princess Dolenta in being named the heir."

I squeezed toothpaste onto a brush and frowned at that. "Why? What's wrong with the kid?"

Mac hummed. "She isn't bloodthirsty enough, I think. According to some gossip links I intercepted, she has an affinity with nature that makes her too soft and reclusive for ruling."

"Who do they want to take her place?"

"Unknown. Her father has an affinity for blood. If it's living, he can control it. It helps that he's ruthless and rules with an iron fist. His marriage was unconventional—ah, did you know Krozalians can only reproduce with a mate? When his wife died, so did any possibility for other heirs."

"That's…I didn't know the Krozalian population was sparse."

Mac guffawed. "Oh, it isn't. Krozalia has a population of around a hundred billion. They're incredibly long-lived. The life span of an average Krozalian is around seven centuries, double that if they're a mated pair. Statistics give one mate-match compatibility per every ten million Kroz. The fertility issue is mostly an issue for pure-blood Krozalians, however. A Kroz can reproduce more easily with other races, but it dilutes their bloodline—hence the reason not every Kroz out there can wield magic, even if they can sense it."

"I think Ravi explained it to me. He classified that as passive and active magic."

"Yes, most Krozalians have passive magic, but only a fraction can shape it at will, all of whom are pure-bloods."

"I'm assuming it's taboo for the emperor to marry from another race to produce more heirs?"

"You assume correctly."

"So who inherits the throne if the emperor and the princess are no longer?" I asked, stomping my feet back into my mag boots.

"Apparently there's a list of obstacles the candidates need to go through to be elected for the position in the event the ruling family has no heir left. In the end, three will compete against each other. Winner takes the throne."

"What about Gamat Com? Did you find anything for Leo?"

"As a matter of fact, I did," Mac said smugly. "It's a galaxy-wide system of interconnected networks currently going by BumbleBee, BlackHole, WhiteStar, among a few others."

I hissed. "What are you saying? Those are—"

"All the networks available out there," Mac finished. "That's right. Gamat Com is the parent company of all those little giants the galaxy can't function without. And it's owned and controlled by the Kroz."

"Were you able to gain access?"

"Not yet," Mac said, and there was a hint of frustration in his voice.

"That changes things," I said.

"I know."

"Leo would make a fortune if he got unrestricted access to it," I mused.

"I thought so too. Endless identities with reliable backgrounds that can't be proven fake, confidential information for blackmail material, and much more at the tip of his fingers. His business would boom. It will attract all sorts of unsavories, and Leo is not savvy enough to evade them. The law, maybe, but mercenaries would hunt him and kill him for it. I don't think we should allow him access to it."

"Mm-hmm. We'll revisit that if you can worm in."

"When."

"Yeah. That." I ran my fingers through my hair and began braiding. "Was there anything else?"

Mac chuffed. "Honey, there's so much info here, it would take me days to finish updating you. I'll spare you the info dump and feed you on a need-to-know basis."

"All right," I said, heading for the door. "I'd like you to look into the fight with the Voner pirate ships and see if you can find anything odd. They weren't cruising that area and came upon us by accident."

"It was an ambush."

"I know. But who orchestrated it? The CTF, the Brofils, someone else? What do they have to gain? Who else knew we'd be traveling to Krozalia through Dante's gateway? I didn't exactly put up a schedule anywhere, and I don't think Ravi did either."

"I thought about that. I ran multiple scanners and the ship came back clean. However they tracked us, it wasn't through a beacon."

***

Once I finished breakfast—three jumbo protein bars—I prepared a mug of tea. Instead of taking it to the bridge the way I always did, I paused by the gym and stuck my head inside. I wanted to have a few words with Sullivan, to see if I could pick his brains about their mission, if they were truly onboard for full crew support, or if they had an ulterior secret mission.

But Sullivan wasn't there. Ravi and Thern were sparring, both wearing nothing but tight drawstring pants that left nothing to the imagination, chest gleaming with sweat. I gawked a few seconds before giggling brought my attention to the other side, where Dolenta and Cassandra sat playing chess. Cassandra waved me over and I headed their way, lowering myself beside them on the mats.

"Hey, Caps. You okay? Sullivan said you crashed after the attack."

"Just needed some rest," I said. "I'm all good now."

Cassandra studied me for a few seconds. "Sunny said you're even better than you used to be. You've been practicing?"

"I'm a one-woman crew without affiliation. I'm not safe from space pirates trying to score. Of course I practice." My eyes slid over at the grappling men. I admired the play of muscles in Ravi's naked back, the way his tattoo seemed to be moving with his every motion.

Cassandra grunted. "I took inventory while you were getting your beauty sleep. Everything is working fine. This baby may be old, but you've taken good care of her."

"Tell her thank you," Mac said.

"Thank you," I repeated and snuck another look at Ravi.

"There were more weapon chutes than this model originally came with. Who did your installments?"

"A friend," I said and waved a hand in dismissal.

"They did a good job. Why all the power? You run into trouble a lot?"

I smirked. She was fishing, and she wasn't being all that subtle about it. "Didn't you just hear me? Vacuum is a place riffling with pirates and thieves. I like to be prepared. I'm armed and dangerous." I flexed my biceps and Dolenta giggled.

Cassandra's eyes remained serious. "You've always been dangerous. It's why the CTF made you captain fresh off the academy."

I sighed. "What do you want me to say, Cassie? I work for myself. I wasn't lying about that."

"If you say so," she grumbled. But she obviously didn't believe me.

"I say so," I affirmed.

My eyes seemed to have developed a mind of their own, because they kept straying to where the two Kroz Warriors sparred, their movements like a dance: elegant and captivating.

Why haven't I ever come to watch them? Cassandra had told me their sparring sessions were a sight to behold. Deep inside, though, I knew. Ravi was a distraction that could get me killed, and it was better for everyone if I kept my distance.

Something inside me had changed the moment Ravi had brushed his lips on mine. The potential of something grand, a life-changer, a new path to choose from the otherwise straight road I'd been traveling through for a long time.

"They've been at that for the past twenty minutes, non-stop," Cassandra said. "They're well matched, and it could take up to an hour before one or both call quits or get in a lucky hit."

"Mmm."

"Which one are you watching?" Cassandra asked.

I cast her a sidelong look. "Both." But only one had my interest piqued.

She chuckled. "I meant which one caught your fancy. Though I'd say both work for me."

I snorted. "I see you're still a flirt."

"Sadly, neither has flirted back," she said wistfully.

"They wouldn't," Dolenta said. "They consider themselves on duty."

Consider this me showing my interest, came Ravi's words in my head. Had his interest come after I'd pointed the lack, or had it been there all along, but professionalism kept him from showing it?

Splendor's Orbit

"On another topic," Cassandra began. "Those ten years treated you well. You haven't changed a bit."

"More than you'll ever know. Images are deceiving." My tone was mild, but I regretted the words the moment they left my mouth.

Her eyes lowered, but not before I saw the shame and guilt. "I'm sorry we left you."

"You didn't have a choice. Sullivan told me what Lorenzo did, how he locked you guys out of the bridge and took control of the ship."

"I wasted time banging on that door. I wasted time pleading for him to listen, not to leave. I could have blitzed the system and overridden the codes. I did nothing." She met my eyes again. "If it was one of us down there, you'd have blown a hole in that door and crawled through. You'd have found a way. Hell, if it hadn't been for Alex, you wouldn't have been delayed in the first and the mission would have gone down smoothly. It was supposed to be a basic go-in, get-out task with no complications."

I swallowed. I'd never tried to see things from their point of view, never wondered if they'd had a reason to leave or not. And I'd always carried this resentment inside me.

Some of the resentment had loosened at Sullivan's explanation the day they'd boarded, and the rest dissipated like smoke in the face of Cassandra's obvious regret. I hated that she'd carried this guilt with her for this long. I squeezed her knee.

"You're right. I got delayed because of Alex and I wouldn't have left him. But I got hurt, and he refused to leave me. Because of that, Alex is gone, and I spent the next couple of years barely hanging to life. I don't blame you for following orders. I'm glad you did."

The metallic tang of blood and ozone, the shouted commands, the floating dust in the air—it all inundated my senses for a few brief seconds. The radio silence from Alex, going back to look for him, being trapped under the rubble.

Snarling at Sullivan to leave, the knowledge we wouldn't make it back to the ship in time, the desperate search for a place to hide before the final detonation went off.

A hand on my shoulder brought me back from my thoughts. "I'm sorry," Cassandra murmured. "I didn't mean to dredge up the memories."

Her eyes shimmered with tears and questions, but she didn't shed or voice them. Probably because she knew I'd already revealed more than I was comfortable sharing.

Dolenta had her face turned as if to give us the illusion of space, but Ravi and Thern had stopped sparring and were watching us. Watching me.

I loosened the fist I hadn't known I'd made and stood. With a small nod to Ravi and a murmured excuse to Cassandra and Dolenta, I left the gym and headed to the bridge, where I found both Lorenzo and Sullivan. Anger, scorching hot and unreasonable, erupted inside me. "Out," I snapped, not caring that I needed to question one or both about their mission on this trip.

Lorenzo opened his mouth, no doubt to spew crap, and I pointed a finger at him. "Get out before I lock you in your room for the rest of the journey."

I hadn't told Cassandra the truth—I hadn't told Sullivan the truth, even when I'd had plenty of chances to do so on this trip.

Cassandra had been the one supposed to come with me that day into the Genesis Facility to plant the explosives, but she'd had a stomach ache and Alex had accompanied me instead. We were supposed to go in, plant the explosives, and then leave.

The Genesis Facility was supposed to have been just a simple facility that some human research and development agency had set up near Sector 9 to conduct scientific studies. It was supposed to be a temporary building, but the moment Alex and I had stepped in, it had felt…like a permanent structure, built for long-term use. That had been our first red flag. The second had come at the obvious way the place had been emptied out in a

Splendor's Orbit

hurry. And then there was the basement.

The underground level had been left out from the debriefing, something Alex and I had chalked to oversight even though the bullshit had been strong enough that we could have smelled it through the EVA suits.

Lorenzo took a step forward, breaking me from the past. "You wouldn't dare," he said through gritted teeth.

"Ooh," Mac said. "He didn't."

I bared my teeth in a faux smile. *I would love nothing more than to dare.*

Lorenzo had tricked Sullivan and Cassandra out of the bridge and then hijacked the ship back to base. He hadn't known Alex and I were both goners. He'd been a coward who wanted to run, and he'd done that.

All my memories were flashing in my head, the pain, the despair, the months spent as a test subject. And the person my emotions blamed for all that hurt was right there, sneering at me, daring me. Sullivan must have seen the violence brewing in my eyes, because he grabbed Lorenzo's wrist and pulled the commodore behind him, sputtering and demanding he be released.

"Maybe next time," Mac comforted.

I took the captain's chair and fiddled with the screen, checking our trajectory, the time stamps on arrival, our journey, and the FTL drive charge. They were nothing but mindless tasks, unnecessary because Mac would have warned me about glitches, or answered any questions I had. But he let me be, aware that I needed the time to compose myself.

"You have company," Mac said. "Should I lock the bridge or let him in?"

I didn't ask who it was, and I debated long enough to make Mac's question a moot point.

Ravi slid into the co-pilot's chair and checked the port view screen. Monitoring the endless black was something else I did, the unbreakable monotony helping to empty my thoughts. He didn't try making small talk, and neither did I.

"Some ships just appeared on the starboard side," Mac said a few minutes later. "They don't look like pirates, but they don't look like Kroz ships either. Tap."

I obeyed and tapped on my screen, and Mac brought the image into view. Three ships, moving in military formation: one ahead and two behind in a triangle shape. I brought the image up into the port view.

"Are these your escort?" I asked.

Ravi cocked his head as he studied the ships. "I can't see an insignia, but they're not royal ships."

I grunted. "I was afraid you were going to say that."

"It doesn't mean they're hostile. They could simply be coming to Dante's Gateway."

"I thought you said that gateway wasn't well used."

"I said that only a handful of people had the code to double jump."

"True," Mac said. "But Dante's Gateway is listed as no longer in use. At least to the public."

I pursed my lips and began mapping a detour. "There's no reason we need to risk being seen"

"Mmm," was Ravi's reply as he tapped on his screen, eyes scanning. "They seem to be coming from the direction of Krozalia—if their trajectory is any indication. Do you have any gamma ray probe in this ship to track their path?"

I raised an eyebrow at that, though my stomach gave a nervous twinge. The *Splendor* did have a gamma ray probe—which was actually what Mac used to detect the ionizing radiation emitted by the thrusters of other ships.

"The *Splendor* is just a freighter and passenger ship."

Ravi snorted. "You have an impressive long-range view for a freighter and passenger ship," he murmured as he studied the screen. "Those ships are billions of kilometers away."

"A little over five hours at the speed they're traveling," I muttered as I brought up the specs. The detour would add about two or three days to our journey, but those were nothing when you were traveling through deep-space.

Ravi's expression turned thoughtful. "There aren't many ships in the Krozalia system outside the army that can maintain that speed."

"You're sure those aren't military Kroz responding to your request for an escort?" I tried again. "Maybe they thought it would be more—discreet to send non-descript ships."

"I don't think so. They'd have sent an encrypted beacon to let us know they would be early."

Once our route had been mapped and the *Splendor* began changing course, I flicked on the intercom. "This is Captain Lee. I want everyone strapped down within five minutes. Remain in your seats until I say otherwise."

A moment later, Lorenzo's voice came through. "Report, captain."

I had the childish urge to ignore him but pushed it away. "Possible hostiles incoming. I've altered course a hundred and eighty degrees around their route."

"Are there any insignias or identification marks?"

"Negative."

"Have you checked with Blackbird?"

"It's next on the list."

I waited a few seconds for a complaint, an order, or any idiotic comment, but for once, Lorenzo made none.

I sent Blackbird an update and then leaned back. "You think they have seen us?" I wondered aloud, though I was really asking Mac.

"If they've been scanning with long-range cameras like yours, maybe," Ravi said.

"We weren't on range yet," Mac replied, and I relaxed. Just a tiny bit. My ship's illegal upgrades were above standard, but it was Mac's diligence that allowed me to catch those details early enough to make a difference.

There was still that possibility of incoming unfriendlies, and for the coming few hours, I remained half-tense in my seat, waiting for Mac to announce the ships had shifted course and were heading our way. I kept monitoring the three red dots on the screen, expecting them to blink out when they hopped closer. But they moved on, not deviating from their paths, or slowing or increasing their speed.

Only when the *Splendor's* long-range radar lost track of their signature did I begin to relax.

"I think I found something," Mac said and I stiffened. "It's a bit disconcerting."

"What?" I breathed.

Ravi glanced at me. "Did you say something?"

"There might be something more to the incident with the pirate ships," Mac said.

"No."

"No, what?" Mac asked.

"I wasn't talking to you," I said. I meant to do it subvocally, but by the way Ravi was eyeing me as if I'd hit my head and loosed some screws, I guessed I'd spoken that aloud. I offered him a faint smile. "Don't mind me, I talk to myself sometimes." His eyebrows winged up, but he didn't say anything.

"Yeah, go ahead and give him that deranged smile you make whenever you're eating chocolate, too," Mac chortled.

I gritted my teeth and waved a hand. "You might want to go assure the princess that it was a false alarm."

"Thern is with her."

Before I could make up a new excuse for him to leave the bridge, Mac projected out the recording of the fight with the pirate ships on the screen. "I'd like his opinion too," Mac said in my ear. "Let him watch."

"What's this?" Ravi asked.

"The recording of the fight with the Voner pirates," I said.

"You might want to look like you're tapping on the screen for this," Mac said, and I began randomly tapping on my console, feeling like a fool and half-expecting the projection ahead to go haywire. That was exactly why I didn't have a crew.

The image zoomed in, catching the moment when Eagle

Splendor's Orbit

13 had dived into the fight, KEW firing at the pirate ships as it expertly maneuvered around the return fire.

The screen zoomed in closer, and I scanned the fight for something that had raised Mac's hackles, so to speak. Eagle 13 was very good. It flew around the pirate ships, dodging fire with an agility that almost matched my own. It did take some hits as the flashing shield suggested, but it didn't stay put long enough for the Voner to lock on it.

"What are you looking for?" Ravi asked just as Eagle 13's shield flashed and fell.

"Tap," Mac said and I did, twice over in the same spot, but I didn't care, and it wasn't as if Ravi was looking at me. The recording rewound a few seconds, then slowed. We saw Blackbird evade an attack and let loose a stream of kinetic fire—hitting Eagle 13 and bringing down their shield. It looked like an accident, but stealth fighters were supposedly highly trained. The best in the field. I had been on track to becoming the youngest stealth fighter pilot the Confederacy had ever seen before things went downhill with the Genesis Mission.

Neither Ravi nor I said anything as the recording resumed playing at normal speed. My fingers flexed, instinct telling me to do something, but logic knew there was nothing that would make a difference now.

Mac knew that as unlikely as it seemed, this wasn't enough to condemn Blackbird for any wrongdoing. So, he either wanted me to be wary—which I was—or something else was going to happen onscreen.

The recording continued, and now that I was aware of what to look for, I kept an eye on the stealth ships. I ignored when Eagle 13 downed a pirate ship a few seconds later, but Mac didn't pause or slow the feed, so I kept my eyes on the second ship. And then, it happened.

Blackbird ducked two blasts from both pirate ships, coming up right behind Eagle 13…and fired.

The blast hit Eagle 13 right where the engines should have been. The feed slowed as Eagle 13 exploded into particles and released oxygen. Because vacuum snuffed out oxygen like a drop of water fired at the sun, explosions in space weren't a grand affair filled with balls of flame and light. No, just sparks here and there, quickly gutted as the gases dispersed.

In a fraction of a second, Eagle 13 was no more. There one second, gone the next, reduced to nothing but debris and pieces of scrap, destined to float in space, forevermore.

As captain of my squad and pilot for the Confederacy for four years, I knew that stealth ships were piloted by elite soldiers with the greatest number of logged hours on active duty. To become a member of one, they had to serve at least ten years as a fleet soldier. Not one member on either ship wasn't qualified to be there—not the captain, navigator, or engineer. Everyone would have received intense training and more hours in the field than any other soldier in any other position on any other ship.

Being hit by friendly fire once was one thing. Being hit twice was something else altogether. Not that I believed that the first time had been a mistake, not when one blast had downed the ship's shield, and the second, which, after rewinding and playing the feed once more, told me that it had been strategically aimed to hit the ship where it was most vulnerable.

Fitting that piece and the pirate ship's sudden departure into the puzzle gave me a new perspective. One I didn't like at all.

"Is your government working with the Voners?" Ravi asked in a calm voice.

"Or Blackbird," I said. There was no love lost between the Confederacy and me, but I couldn't just throw the whole government into the same box of suspicion as Blackbird.

"It's highly suspicious that we were attacked on Cyrus station by Brofil mercenaries when the Confederacy and Brofils had scheduled an enclave there. And now this."

I said nothing. I had nothing to say. Not in anyone's defense. Obviously, there was much more to the story than we were seeing, and Ravi seemed to understand that too. He unfastened his harness and stood. "I'd appreciate it if you sent me a copy of that recording."

"Where are you going?" I asked. "What are you going to do?"

"I'm going to have a talk with my second, and then we're going to see Commodore Lorenzo."

Chapter 19

Lord Drax

I paused the recording as the fragmented remains of Eagle 13 dispersed into the cosmos and looked at Thern.

"They can't be the mole," he murmured, a deep furrow on his brow. "How could they have known where we'd be?"

"I don't know. But you know how I feel about coincidences. At the moment, the Confederacy is the only common denominator in this whole mess." I gritted my teeth at the possibility of a traitor on this ship. "I'm going to have a hard talk with Commodore Lorenzo. Someone put the two stealth crews together, and Admiral Fulk was adamant we have an escort. Whose idea was it? Who picked the stealth fighters? I want answers, even if I have to force them from him."

"No," Thern said sharply. "If you corner him and they're guilty, they will have no choice but to react. Like it or not, we're currently at their mercy. We'll watch them closer and try to stay a step ahead."

I clenched and unclenched my fists. "If they're in on this, I can take the three of them."

"Not if the stealth fighter is taking orders from any of them. If they're on a scheduled report around the clock, the moment they fail to communicate, Blackbird could attack."

"Not if we attack them first," I said, confident that the *Splendor* could defeat Blackbird. The only problem would be convincing the captain to do it.

"What about Captain Lee?"

I dragged my attention from the plan forming in my head and focused on Thern's words. "What about her?"

"She's more likely to be the spy."

"No." I glared at him. "She's not."

"Are you telling me she couldn't backstab us?"

"She's been fighting for us since we reached Cyrus Station."

"She could have staged the attack."

I recalled the way she'd fought the Brofils, the subsequent dangerous rush to get us away, the way she'd fought the pirates—merciless, competent, not giving an inch.

"You didn't see what she did. Damn, Thern! If you'd seen the way she fought three Voner ships, you'd be foaming at the mouth to get her into our aerial fleet."

Thern shrugged, unimpressed. But I knew if he'd seen the fight, if he'd been in the bridge then, he wouldn't cast any suspicion toward the elfin female. Or maybe he would.

"I'm just saying. This is just a passenger ship and not even a new model. You've fought the Voner before. You know how good they are. She shouldn't have been able to eliminate one, much less three of them. Maybe this is all a setup for us to trust her." He raised a hand when I opened my mouth to protest. "Remember how adamant she was not to take us on this journey?"

I scoffed. "You can't have it both ways, if this was a setup, she wouldn't have tried to reject our offer and run."

"I'm playing with both sides so we can consider all the possibilities. We were told she was the best, and we skipped all the more reputable and well-known companies in lieu of discretion. Remember it was her decision to take us to Cyrus Station for food we could have bought at V-5. You only told her about Dante's Gateway after we were on our way from Cyrus, and yet, we were ambushed there not by one, not two, but seven Voner pirate ships. They knew where we'd be and what time we'd be there. Even the other humans were muttering about the coincidence."

"It wasn't the captain," I said, though my voice lacked conviction.

Thern placed a hand on my shoulder and squeezed. "I've noticed the way you watch this female. I know you don't want to believe the worst about her."

"She's a mate-match," I said quietly.

That shocked Thern enough to shut him up. "You're kidding. A human?"

I rubbed a hand over my chest. "I know. I mean, I don't know. It's just, I feel things, instinctive things for her that are out of character for me."

Thern winced. "If you ignore the urges that you feel are out of character, it'll discourage the bond."

Disappointment panged dully inside me. He was right. Just because we were compatible didn't mean I had to act on it. I gave Thern a small smile and my insides curdled with the decision. "You're right. It still doesn't mean that she's the mole."

"Think about it," Thern said earnestly. "The Confederacy came after the Brofil mercenaries. Before that, the princess and I were taken from the ship without any effort. Who gave them the means to disable the ship, walk in, and catch the princess and me unaware long enough to drug us?"

"You forget she was the one who tracked and fought for you."

"Yes, and didn't that make us trust her more?" He raised his hand beseechingly and then let it drop again. "By the stars, Ravi, maybe this isn't about the princess. Maybe the people who attacked our ship believe we were killed with the rest. Maybe this is a scheme concocted by the Confederacy—this capture and rescue thing, to make us more amenable to their negotiations. Why do they want the KKM trade? Did you manage to get a straight answer from the admiral? Its amplifying abilities can be used in so many things that can later be employed against us." Thern's eyes turned sympathetic. "Have you even reviewed the information cube that Admiral Fulk gave you?"

He knew I hadn't. I pursed my lips and looked down at my clenched fists. There was a reason why I'd chosen Thern as my second, and it wasn't only for his combative skills and magic mastery, but the way he could strategize on his feet. As much as my gut told me he was wrong, I couldn't dismiss all the points he'd just made. I did want the captain to be innocent in all this—all her actions to date pointed to her being the hero, but maybe I needed to step back and read between the lines.

The information cube I'd requested from Admiral Fulk was still locked in my bunk. I hadn't wanted to taint my opinion of the captain—whoever she'd been ten years ago didn't matter today—but I couldn't afford to ignore it any longer.

It was time for me to read her military file.

I met Thern's eyes. "You're right. I let my attraction taint my perception. I'll make sure it doesn't happen again. Not until I can clear the captain and the princess is back home."

A flash of sadness crossed Thern's expression, but I turned and left his bunk before he could give me empty platitudes.

Chapter 20

"You think Lorenzo knows about this?" I asked Mac as the door to the bridge slid shut behind Ravi.

"Maybe. There are countless scenarios and possibilities to consider. We simply don't have sufficient information to make any solid assumptions."

"What about Blackbird?"

"I'm keeping my eyes on them. The moment I get any offensive reading, I'll blow that tin can out of existence."

I grunted. The *Splendor's* weapons, like the controls, were the only two things Mac couldn't manipulate. But he'd let me know the moment he sensed any hostile changes on Blackbird, and I wouldn't hesitate to react on his say so. "I don't like the look in Ravi's eyes. Why didn't you wait until he'd gone before displaying the recording?"

"I want to see what he'll do and what the reaction will be. I need more information. Those Voners weren't fighting for keeps, they were fighting to destroy."

I scratched my head as I considered his words, tugged on a lock of hair, then shook my head. "Whatever this is, I think we should have handled it without the Kroz's interference. The only people hurt are the members of Eagle 13, and they were all human." I'd been a soldier long enough to know that you didn't throw a fellow soldier over the barrel for personal grievances.

"Were you a bit slower, we could have suffered Eagle 13's fate a dozen times over."

I grimaced. If Mac said a dozen times, then he meant exactly that. That number wasn't a guess or an exaggeration, but a mathematical equation he'd calculated after our fight.

I exhaled. "Okay, keep an eye on him and let me know the moment his conversation with Lorenzo heats up."

Because it would heat up, and not just a little. It would get scorching. If I were in Ravi's place, I'd probably be shoving Lorenzo into an airlock. Hell, I was in his place, considering I and my ship could have been blown to space debris just as easily. But even as the thought crossed my mind I knew it wasn't true. Lorenzo was an asshole, always tromping on people to climb to the top, but he wasn't a traitor, wasn't a backstabber. He had an agenda. I believed that, but it was to climb as high as possible in the CTF and to be the best there was to impress mommy dearest. Killing me or my passengers wouldn't get him anywhere. Besides, he was a selfish son of a bitch. He'd never sacrifice himself for the good of anyone, or anything, else.

And the CTF wouldn't risk an intergalactic war with the Kroz. They were already struggling to fend off the Cradox, and the Cradox's might paled in comparison to the sheer strength of the Kroz.

Attacking the *Splendor* when the princess was aboard would achieve nothing good, and the CTF knew that.

With that new thought in mind, sharing our findings with Lorenzo was a wise course of action. A conclusion Ravi had already reached. Whatever Lorenzo's faults, he was a commodore, and with him lay answers.

I was about to head out to speak with Lorenzo when Mac's voice sounded in my ear. "You won't believe what I found!"

"What now?" I asked warily.

"I had a comb running for our Mr. Ravi Drax, trying to find out more about our illustrious passenger and—"

"Oh, good grief, you're not still hacking their government files, are you? Tell me you're not."

"Fine, if you want me to lie to you. But I should first remind you that you detest liars. You have a 3.2 percent tolerance for liars and cheats."

I ignored that last part, aware he was trying to distract

me. "How do you know you didn't trip any alarms?" I demanded. "You said it yourself their system is different from anything you've ever seen. I thought you'd do the reasonable thing and stop trying to hack it."

"I didn't trip any alarm." If he was a person, he'd be raising his chin in stubborn pride, right now.

I sighed and let my head fall back into the headrest. "What did you find?" I asked, eyes closed.

"Maybe I don't want to tell you anymore. Maybe you're not worthy of all the Intel I can gather. Maybe we should ask Baltsar to root me out and implant my matrix in someone who doesn't question my capabilities."

"Mac."

"Fine. But brace yourself. What I found will knock you back so hard, you'll get whiplash—"

I gritted my teeth. "Mac."

"Fine, fine. Our esteemed passenger, Ravi Drax, isn't just a security detail, but in fact Madrovi Fidraxi, Krozalia's head guard, the emperor's left hand, and…hold onto your breeches: he's also the Grim Reaper of the Galaxy."

My breath exploded as if I'd just been sucker punched in the stomach.

"I know. The man you're making moon eyes at is the person you'd be brought to for public execution should your mods ever be discovered. Personally, I think your luck must have been lost somewhere during our last trip. No one's that unfortunate."

I rubbed a shaky hand over my mouth. "You're sure about that?" I asked even though I knew Mac wouldn't have told me before checking and re-checking the facts more than once.

"Please, I'm not a fifty-year-old garbage piece someone put together from a junkyard in a disposable asteroid cave."

After going through a dozen ways having the Grim Reaper on board my ship could end with my death, I forced myself to think reasonably. Ravi wasn't here because he knew about all my enhancements and modifications; he wasn't here because he was investigating genetically enhanced humans. He was here as a passenger, a client, a bodyguard to the Princess of Krozalia. Really, I should have guessed this sooner had I not been so preoccupied with everything else. Who better to protect the princess than the one most feared in the galaxy, the Kroz who could unmake a person with the wave of a hand? Whoever Ravi was in Krozalia, here, on my ship, he was simply a bodyguard. There was nothing I could do but to make sure they reached Dupilaz Moon without any more incidents—and to hold on tighter to my secrets.

With those reassuring thoughts in my head, I calmed down from the brink of a full-blown panic attack. I was going to limit contact with the Kroz and get us to Dupilaz Moon, then get out of dodge with utmost haste.

My resolve had just settled around me like a comforting blanket when I received more bad news.

"Incoming," Mac said, projecting the view outside into the port view screen.

Three ships like the ones we'd changed course to avoid earlier were approaching. The numbers showed they were still far, but with their speed, our paths would cross in less than two hours.

"They're much closer than the last three," I observed, scrutinizing the ships for any distinguishing marks or registration numbers and finding none.

"That's the thing," Mac said, and although he was an AI created in a dark lab, I could hear a grim note in his voice. "They hopped to that location."

I sucked in a breath. "They could be heading to Dante's Gateway," I said, but I didn't believe that. Once, I could accept as a coincidence. Twice was something else altogether.

"We'll change course and go around them," I said and reached for the intercom. "This is Captain Lee," I began. "Please strap in. We're on an intersecting course with three unknown ships. I'm changing course, but they might have already spotted us."

I turned the coms off and returned my attention to the port view image Mac was still displaying, along with all estimations and statistics.

"How's our ballistic ammo?" I asked. My gut was telling me we were going to need every weapon we possessed to survive this.

"Our lasers are fully charged," Mac began, then his voice switched to my ear, letting me know we had company. "We still have approximately three thousand long shells for the turrets."

I grunted. We hadn't used them last time. They weren't as effective on a hull as laser and kinetic fire.

A moment later, the door swished open, and in came Ravi, along with Sullivan. I ignored both and scanned the data scrolling on the screen. "KEW is at seventy-two percent. The plas cannon can fire three long bolts, or five smaller ones before it needs recharging."

"Shields?" I asked sub-vocally.

"Primary is at fifty-six capacity and secondary at ninety-eight."

"I want those shields at maximum capacity. Use the remaining charge from the FTL if necessary."

Although there was nothing indicating any threats yet, my gut was heavy with imminent doom.

We were all surveilling the three ships on the screen, so the moment they disappeared, I raised the alarms and flicked on the ship's shield, even though the readings told me we were still at sixty-one percent capacity.

My reflex saved us from joining vacuum dust, because three seconds after the ships disappeared, they appeared again, this time within striking distance.

Two laser blasts fired from the *Splendor*. "Take that, you fuckers!" Sullivan snarled and punctuated that with two more blasts. And then my fears came true. Three more ships suddenly blipped into existence behind us, probably the same ones I'd changed our course to avoid.

A stream of creative expletives escaped Sullivan's mouth

Splendor's Orbit

just as a hail of laser fire rained our way.

I dipped the ship down and punched our speed to maximum without engaging the FTL and spiraled away, dodging fire left and right. We took some hits, our primary shield's capacity decreasing with each, but there was nothing to do but dodge, thrust, and dodge again.

I primed the plas cannon, and Sullivan gasped. Up to that point, he'd only known about the lasers and kinetic fire, and although it wasn't common for a freight ship to be armed, it still wasn't that uncommon. But plas cannons were a category of their own, mostly found in battleships ten times the size of the *Splendor*. They were usually the size of a stealth ship, but the *Splendor's* plas cannon was a portable model that I had salvaged from a cradoxian mining asteroid two years ago.

I felt, rather than saw, Ravi's heavy gaze fixed on me, but I ignored him, ignored Sullivan's mutterings, and anything else that wasn't directly related to the fight we were facing.

What was that old saying—bad news came in threes? Only ours came times three.

Ravi started punching numbers and plotting courses into my screen. I'd be faster merging with Mac, but it hadn't been too long since the last time, and I didn't know if my brain could take it without suffering permanent damage—or risking losing my identity. No one wanted that outcome, not me and certainly not Mac.

I followed the course Ravi set, winding around two ships before coming up behind the enemy and rolling sideways as Sullivan fired so many laser blasts, they were almost one stream. I caught a glimpse of Blackbird engaging two other ships, but that still left me with four. Even with Ravi's fast calculations, we were taking too many hits for my comfort.

The *Splendor's* primary shield was down to sixteen percent; one more hit and it would fall completely. The secondary shield wasn't as hardy. Two, three hits and we'd be naked and vulnerable to the weakest tap.

That decided it. I'd rather risk the chance of losing

myself than the certainty of losing this battle and everyone's lives. With that realization, I allowed my mind to expand, reaching out to Mac and slowly synching with him, even as he linked me to the *Splendor*. Being able to see outside the ship in a 360 degree should have been disorienting, but Mac did something to prevent any wasted time. Still, keeping tabs on all the enemy ships closing in with the intention to obliterate us to dust was a heart-stopping moment.

Statistics ran in my head, and I knew that even merged, our chance of coming out the other side with the hull intact enough to reach Dupilaz Moon was seventeen percent. For a forty-four percent success chance, a full merging with Mac and the ship would be necessary. There was a thirty-eight percent chance I'd survive the merging without any lasting effect and an eighty-one percent that Mac wouldn't be able to erect a buffer between our minds once this was over.

All that flashed in my mind in a nanosecond, along with a myriad of scenarios and outcomes, none with a satisfactory prediction of us getting away alive.

I dodged a laser blast and pushed on with the merging. I'd never pushed this far, and my natural defenses pushed back, trying to protect myself, to preserve my mind. Somewhere in the depths of my soul, alarms blared, but the apathy of my machine and the engine combined kept it to a low thrum, more like white noise. I dug into the *Splendor's* matrix, allowing my body to extend and sync AI and engine together into one cohesive being. By the time we were one, I was flying by instinct, Ravi's fast and strategic navigating course too slow and fallible.

My ship was my body, Mac's computation skills my agility, and I was but the vessel that commanded both.

An enemy ship detached from the fight, and my measurements told me it would try to flank me and drive me into the path of a second ship. It would shoot my shield while the third and the fourth would hem me in and fire from both directions. I flipped and engaged the nose thrusters, causing the *Splendor* to slide ninety degrees sideways.

Splendor's Orbit

I fired the KEW and 24.1 mm bullets. While the ammunition couldn't do much damage to the hull of a ship, it could down a shield faster than energy-based weapons. The ship's shield blinked out, and I fired the plas cannon, aiming for the spot the enemy ship would be in the next three seconds. The problem with cannon fire was that it gave other ships ample time to dodge unless they were caught by surprise. When flying in a vacuum, there were no forces to help a ship to any direction but the ones coming from that ship's engine. Once a certain speed was reached, there were only so many feasible directions to go, and the enemy ship didn't disappoint. It helped that plas fire didn't really need accuracy. Three seconds after the long plas fire launched, it hit the enemy ship starboard and breached the hull.

My energy began to drain like water down a sieve, and with a flicker of emotion, I knew if I wanted to get the *Splendor* away intact, I had to finish the other three ships within five minutes. Assuming, of course, that Blackbird finished the other two.

Ravi was still mapping paths to my private com screen that I ignored, and Sullivan was trying to wrest control of the ship's weapons, but I'd locked him out.

Couldn't have him messing with my aim or crashing my commands. As a result, Sullivan was shouting something in the background that I paid little attention to and Ravi was shouting in Krozalian.

Two of the ships were trying to flank the *Splendor* on either side, and the third was charging from the front. I pulled the ship higher, nose raised in the air, and shot a small burst of the FTL charge. Within the infinite space of a millisecond, I had the computation and outcomes of several attack plans that I discarded, preferring to settle for the simplest. I sped up, then arched back down, coming behind the ship that had been on a collision course with the *Splendor* seconds ago. I fired a multitude of blasts from close up, aware that one of the enemy ships was closing in behind me. I sped ahead and so did the ship behind. The one in front vaulted and flipped around, now facing the *Splendor*—and closing in. It was a dangerous move, but I bet it was one they'd practiced. Playing chicken in vacuum was a dick move. One I'd never backed down from before, and never lost.

A plan formed. I was reaching for the searchlight even before finishing calculating. I blacked out the cameras and all the screens just as a brilliant light flashed outside. Most ships were equipped to filter out sunlight, so all I'd get was the second it took for those filters to come online. I pulled above and to the side of the ship closing in from ahead. A concussive blast hit the *Splendor*. I didn't need to check to know that the two enemy ships had collided.

One ship left and a bit more than three minutes before my body gave out. Our odds had shot up to eighty-three percent.

The data had barely grazed my mind when a dark splotch covered my entire view of space ahead. I pulled the ship sideways and down, but not fast enough. The starboard wing scraped against the dark hull, bringing the *Splendor's* primary shield down and the secondary to seven percent in one go.

But that wasn't what had all my alerts on high. No, it was the fact that the ship the *Splendor* had just kissed was a Class 5 Kroz Battleship.

It was about ten kilometers in diameter, about the size of a small station, with enough power to destroy an entire moon. I'd never seen one in person, but there were plenty of documentaries from the time the Kroz had fought on Earth, centuries ago.

Logic told me they were the escort Ravi had requested, but I was disabused of that notion in the next second.

Several plas cannon ports opened, and all the target-locked alarms of the *Splendor* blared to life.

More than a few plas cannons fired, and I barely managed to escape the two aimed at us by crossing behind the large hull of a destroyed ship. Unfortunately, Blackbird and the other two ships didn't escape the assault. There was a brilliant flash, a spherical fireball, and a lot of unrecognizable debris.

With the field cleared, it was only the *Splendor*, the Kroz battleship, and dead detritus. Our chance to survive this battle was less than a fraction of one percent.

I located every person onboard and sealed them in whatever room they were in with nothing but emergency lights and life support. Anything else was turned off and all the ship's power was reverted to the FTL drive. If I hadn't been this deeply synched with the ship's engine, the whole procedure would have taken me at least four minutes. But with the merging, my thoughts alone were enough to have everything activated and the *Splendor* hopping within five seconds.

Still, not even using all the power on the FTL was enough to get us far from the battleship. Maybe if I hadn't used the charge on the ship's shield, or maybe if we'd gone back to Baltsar for the extra FTL energy boost...but we did and I hadn't, so I really had one desperate choice. What I did next was so reckless I was cringing even as I was doing it—I fed the FTL my own energy. I held on until the flashing light of the hyperjump began filling with dark spots and I was about to pass out. Only then did I bring us out. We'd only spent a little over ten seconds in hyperspace, but it should have been enough to get us a week ahead of schedule.

I didn't have time and energy to check where exactly we would come out, just general computations of a location somewhere in the direction we were going. I hoped I hadn't taken us too far off course. It was hard to calculate course changes with precision during battles, but I'd learned enough in the military to get things rounded to a close substitute.

My question was answered in the next second.

We came out in the middle of an asteroid belt.

I managed to keep us from crashing into the larger rocks long enough for Ravi to plot a path away before darkness consumed me.

Chapter 21

Lord Drax
Helpless.

Never had I been so helpless in my life, the way I had been throughout those frantic minutes during the fight.

My fingers clenched at the memory of how many times we had flirted with death today, at how Captain Lee had locked the navigation system and the weapons so only she commanded the ship.

Admiration and fury fought for supremacy inside me, overshadowed by how incredible she was, her piloting prowess, her fast and strategic mind. Never had I come across a pilot as proficient, and by the shocked disbelief in Sullivan's expression, neither had he. Apparently, Captain Lee had spent the past ten years training. For what and why, was the mystery I intended to solve.

There had been nothing in the info cube Admiral Fulk had given me indicating that the captain was so exceptional. Brave, quick thinking, ambitious, and loyal to a fault had been the words used to describe her. Qualities I'd come by without needing to read the file and intrude on her privacy.

The oldest of three siblings, she'd joined the army at eighteen, already an expert pilot and asset to the Confederacy. She'd risen in the ranks quickly, becoming a captain and leader of her squad at twenty, only to die in action at age twenty-two during a mission on the edges of Sector 9, along with her second and co-pilot, Alex Rubin. I hadn't read the rest of the file, mostly because it had satisfied the doubts Thern had seeded, but also because I wanted to learn more about her through her words and

Splendor's Orbit

her actions, not through the flat words of a military report.

Captain Lee was not involved in any of the incidents we had faced unless I wanted to count her as the savior she was.

A savior who had fallen unconscious for no apparent reason.

I glanced at her, small and vulnerable-looking in the big captain chair, face pale and clammy. Her pulse was fast but strong, and her pupils enlarged, but there was no other apparent reason for her collapse. In the ether, her energy was dimmer than usual, but still vibrant—like a halo around her. Whatever her illness, it wasn't life-threatening.

There hadn't been any medical condition in her military file, and Sullivan claimed not to know either. It meant whatever had caused her collapse was either a new medical condition or something else.

Nothing I can do with the ship locked down this tightly but wait and hope I don't have to command any of the six royal escorts currently surrounding the Splendor *to board and forcefully breach the hull.* Captain Lee wouldn't take kindly to that, I mused, but it was something I'd order done if she didn't wake soon.

Six more escorts had been sent to investigate the battleship that had attacked us, only to report there was nothing but the remains of a violent battle drifting in space. I could tell they were having a hard time believing we'd been attacked by a royal battleship, but no one had voiced their doubts. No one with this kind of clearance should want the princess dead, but they'd done us—me—a favor by attacking in such a manner. Because there were only so many people with a high enough rank to command a battleship. My investigation had narrowed down the list of potential traitors considerably with this latest move. Now, all I needed was to reach Krozalia and review the current roster of nobility with a military background.

If only the captain would awaken so we could speed things up.

I cast her another glance, my thoughts shifting from the

attack to whatever had ailed her. I arranged her body more comfortably in the pilot's chair, then laid her hands atop each other. She was soft and warm. The pang of yearning I felt for this female was unexpected, but not surprising. I'd already decided I'd do everything I could to convince her to come to Krozalia with me, even if I had to concoct a story. I couldn't let her walk away, not without exploring the scope of this pull I felt. Determining if we were indeed a mate-match or if this was just attraction was the first step, and for that, I needed more time with her.

A ceremony of gratitude for her heroic service, perhaps, I considered as I settled back in my seat. I'd insist when she refused—and I knew she would—and imply any refusal to attend would be considered a grave insult directed at the emperor himself. Yes, that would work. With that decided, I settled in to wait for the captain to wake up.

Chapter 22

I was still in the pilot's chair when I awoke. That surprised me. Not because I expected someone to have carried me to bed, but because, well, I'd expected someone would have carried me to bed. Not because I had anticipated affection or tender feelings toward me, but rather that someone would have tried taking the pilot's seat.

I inhaled deeply before shifting and opening my eyes. All the lights were off, save for the red emergency ones. We were still operating on auxiliary power only. No numbers or script filled the screen, not the one for the captain, or the ones on the console. The port view ahead was the dark of space, with a few stars scattered about. If it wasn't for the thrum of the engine through the bridge, I'd have said we were at a standstill.

With that fact gathered, I took inventory of my own body. A lingering low-grade headache buzzed behind my eyes, some sore muscles on my arms and legs, and a fast, erratic heartbeat were the only physical side effects I could tell from a quick assessment.

I straightened from my slump, and my stomach did a quick dive and swim. To my surprise, Ravi was still on the co-pilot's chair—watching me.

"Welcome back, captain," he murmured.

"How—" I swallowed and tried again. "How long was I out?"

He glanced down at his commlink. "Eighteen hours, seventeen minutes, and forty-three seconds."

My eyebrows shot up at the precision. "Where are we?"

"A few days away from Dupilaz Moon."

"The escort?"

"Flanking us." He indicated the proximity screen with his chin, which was when I realized there were six ships around us: two starboard side, two port side, and two more at our rear. They were all showing red, which meant they were still marked as enemy ships.

I tapped to zoom closer, finding the Kroz insignia and registration number at once. I checked all six before switching from enemy to friendly. Not that it meant anything, I thought, recalling the Class 5 Kroz Battleship. They could, for all I knew, turn around and start firing at any moment.

Some of that thought must have shown on my face, because Ravi said, "They're all from my own platoon. I know each person on those ships by name and rank."

I made a non-committal sound in my throat and set up a scanner to identify any damages that had occurred during the fight. I wasn't looking forward to a trip outside, but if anything needed patching, I'd have to do it. I didn't have EVA suits that would fit anyone else aboard the *Splendor*. Save maybe Dolenta.

I began unbuckling my harness. I needed some protein, some water, and to stretch my legs a bit before doing anything else.

"Where are you going?" he asked.

I paused and looked at him. It wasn't the question, but the way he asked it, that had me assessing the ship again. That was when I noticed Sullivan, asleep in the tactical seat, head tilted to one side, mouth slightly agape.

"Um," I began, looking back at the screen. I wanted to reach out to Mac because it had just occurred to me that in the minutes since I'd awoken, he had yet to say anything.

A cold grip of fear tightened my insides as I remembered Baltsar telling me merging with the ship and Mac could cook my brains, destroy the *Splendor's* engine, or fry Mac, if not all three. Because I'd awakened with nothing but minor aches, I'd figured everything else was fine.

Have I finally killed him?

"Mac?" I said sub-vocally, but there was no answer. I swallowed and reached for my screen.

"The ship's been on lockdown since you passed out," Ravi was saying.

I frowned but said nothing. I hadn't accounted that with me and Mac both out, the *Splendor* wouldn't respond to anyone without an override code. I had forgotten to authorize Ravi a temporary admin's pass.

"The only thing that works is that the navigation system responds to the courses I input."

Because he hadn't tried to change it from the original destination, I thought.

"What about the others?" I asked.

"They're all locked down in their bunks."

I winced at that. No wonder Sullivan was asleep in his station—I'd taken all the power from all empty decks to charge the last hop. I began manually compressing the ship again. "I'm sorry," I said.

"Care to tell me what's wrong with you?"

"No."

"This is the second time after a battle that you passed out."

Technically, I hadn't passed out after the first, but I didn't want to discuss this topic with him. I pursed my lips and checked the power charge. Fifteen percent and charging. And that after eighteen hours. I wondered how low we'd gotten. Hopefully, the closer we got to Krozalia's sun, the faster the charge would top off.

"Captain?"

I glanced up and met his eyes. "It's a medical condition. Too much adrenaline causes my body to shut down. The more adrenaline dump, the longer it takes for me to wake up."

Ravi frowned. "I never heard of such a condition," he said.

Neither have I. I shrugged. It probably did exist out there somewhere. In the silence that followed, I reached out to Mac in the void of my mind, where his presence should have been. I was greeted with a piercing headache that caused an involuntary gasp and made my eyes tear up. I doubled over in my seat, clutching my head. Saliva pooled in my mouth and my breathing hitched.

Vaguely, I sensed Ravi crouched beside me, one hand rubbing my back as he spoke words I couldn't decipher.

It took me a while to unclench my body and wipe my cheeks. I wasn't sure if the tears were from pain or Mac's absence; my senses were too scrambled to tell the difference.

"Here." A bottle of water appeared in front of my face, Ravi's long fingers encircling it.

I squinted up at him, the red emergency lights too bright on my sensitive eyes.

But I could detect the worry in Ravi's expression, the questions he wasn't voicing.

I reached for the water. "Thank you," I said and fumbled to crack the seal. The water was cool and refreshing, and it settled my stomach and nerves a bit.

In hindsight, I shouldn't have tried to reach Mac; my psyche was still fragile after the deep merging.

"What was that?" Ravi asked at last.

I opened my mouth to reply, then shut it again and sighed. "Just a side effect. I need to eat and rest a bit more."

The systems chose that moment to come back online, the lights switching from red to soft yellow. I made sure all compartments had sufficient pressure and oxygen. I was about to lift the lockdown when Ravi stopped me.

"Wait," he said, then clamped his mouth shut when I gave him a questioning look.

"Yes?" I prompted.

"Before you release anyone, I need to speak to Thern."

I cocked my head, but didn't need to prompt him to speak.

"Someone on this ship set us up. Someone is leaking information about our location."

I looked away. Mac had said Lorenzo had been sending

out encrypted messages to Dupilaz Moon, but there'd been nothing dangerous, no double meaning. Nothing Mac or I could decipher anyway. Aside from him and Ravi, no one else had sent any messages. But no one had known about the *Splendor's* route—no one that wasn't already on this ship.

"It could have been anyone from the Blackbird," I said.

They were the logical explanation.

Ravi inclined his head. "Yes, that's the more likely scenario. But Blackbird took orders from someone somewhere." He made a dismissive motion with one hand. "This close to our destination, if we're wrong, whoever the mole is, if they're on this ship, they'd be desperate. And desperate people do stupid things."

I pursed my lips. He was right. As much as I hated the notion, I couldn't dismiss it. Besides, it had been ten years since I'd had any interaction with them. People changed—I was a prime example of that. Maybe they thought they were acting for the good of humanity. I could see Cassandra, Sullivan, and maybe even Lorenzo, doing something dramatic for the cause. But killing a child?

I exhaled. "All right."

Ravi stood. "I want to check the ship for possible trackers first. I won't be long." He left, and with a sigh, I reached for the protein bar I kept in the side pocket of my seat, along with another bottle of water.

"I know you're awake," I said. "How much did you hear?"

Sullivan stirred. "Enough. It's not Cassie or Lorenzo."

"I hope not."

"I heard about the adrenaline overload." Sullivan's voice was low, almost embarrassed, and when I turned to face him he wouldn't meet my eyes. "Is that why you didn't come back? We'd work on that. There are counterdrugs you can take. It's not a big deal."

"It's not that," I began.

"What, then? If you tell me, I'll do my best to help."

I sighed. Sullivan had never met a puzzle he didn't want to solve, and he was a dog with a bone, gnawing and gnawing, trying to reach the juicy part.

"I didn't want to go back," I finally said, holding his eyes so he could see how serious I was. "I knew if I let anyone know I was alive that I'd need to get back to duty. I didn't want to be part of a team that follows orders blindly, or wouldn't have my back when things got hard."

Remorse filled Sullivan's eyes, but I plowed on, not wanting him to continue down this path. It would only get me killed, and probably him as well. The scientists had already proven to me, time and again, that they'd kill to keep their secrets, and they didn't care who you were, how many titles or honorifics your name held.

"Knowing what I know now, I still wouldn't go back. I don't blame you for what happened, I get that it wasn't up to you." I huffed a humorless laugh. "I know had you wrestled Lorenzo from the bridge and stayed, you'd be just as dead as Alex, so I'm glad Lorenzo got you guys out of there. I told Alex to go, but he refused. We had no time to get back to the ship, so I planned to seek cover behind a rock wall I'd spotted going in, hoping it would protect us from the worst of the debris.

"Things blew up before we got there, and we were flung into the vacuum. I don't remember much about what followed, only glimpses of endless black, but I didn't die from oxygen deprivation, so the salvage ship that got us out must have found us before my EVA suit ran out. When I awoke next, I was in Delta-1, and seven months had passed."

"And Alex?"

"He died before they could get him the help he needed." I rubbed my hands together. They were freezing cold, a sign that I needed more protein. "It took me months more to function again. I had to train myself to walk, to hold a spoon, to speak simple words. The day I left, I was a new person, and Clara Colderaro was dead."

It was a much-abbreviated truth, but more than I'd

planned to tell him. I'd been taken by a salvage ship, but they'd been sent by the scientists to see if they could salvage anything. I'd been taken to Delta-1, a pirate station where the only law was not to damage the structure and to keep any strife away from the streets and the public. I'd been unconscious for months while my right side was replaced with inorganic matter. At some point, the scientists had taken me to Raptune planet for the AI installation and programming phase of my new life. I was the perfect specimen for the scientists: healthy, young, fit, and presumably dead. It had taken months for me to learn to walk on my new, mechanical leg and use my improved arm and fingers, to process thoughts and equations by commanding the newly implanted AI in my nervous system.

"I'm sorry," Sullivan said softly. "If we'd known you survived—"

"You didn't, and command wouldn't have let you return. We fucked up that mission, and Alex and I paid for it. It happened, it's in the past. No amount of remorse will change that. Now, please leave. The galley is unlocked. I'm sure you'd love something to eat after all these hours stuck here."

"You're wrong," Sullivan said as he stood. "Maybe if we'd stayed, we would have managed to get you and Alex into the ship in time. Maybe we'd have found you and Alex floating and put you in the med unit fast enough your wounds wouldn't have been so severe. Maybe we would have come closer and gotten you away without your need to run and hide."

"You don't know—"

"No, I don't," he said harshly. "And neither do you."

"Just go," I said, quiet enough that it was easy to miss.

But I knew he hadn't. I could tell he was standing there, undecided and wanting to say more. I closed my eyes. Whether Sullivan gave me a list of potential outcomes for that day or not, nothing would change. I was here, Alex was not, the scientists were out there. No amount of wishing and probabilities would change that.

At long last, Sullivan's footsteps started fading away. I

glanced back when his steps stopped and found Ravi by the door. Umber eyes met mine, and my stomach sank. I didn't want to talk to him. Not the man he was posing to be, and certainly not the galaxy's judge, jury, and executioner.

Maybe he read something from my expression, because he moved back, giving room for Sullivan to pass.

"Do you want to talk about it?" Ravi asked as he walked in.

"No. Did you find anything?"

"No," he said. "But I haven't searched the whole ship yet. I want Thern to help. Could you unlock only his bunk?"

I stood. "Let's go."

Chapter 23

Lord Drax

I waited as the captain entered the override code for Thern's bunk. She was pale, paler than she'd been when she'd been unconscious, sweat beading on her hairline and upper lip.

She wasn't fine. Something unrecognizable stirred inside me, along with the urge to do something to help.

The red light on the panel turned green and the captain looked up at me, feigned a smile that didn't reach her eyes, and turned to go. I reached out and grabbed her arm, preventing her from leaving. "Will you be okay?" I asked.

The surprise in her eyes when I grabbed her faded to warmth. "I just need some protein and rest."

I searched her face for something, any hint of what ailed her, and found no clue. So I released her, but she didn't immediately go.

She opened her mouth just as the door to Thern's room slid open. There came the sound of a weapon discharging. I watched, seemingly in slow motion, as the captain was propelled back with the force of the impact. She hit her head on the unforgiving bulkhead and slid down, unconscious. It took me precious seconds to comprehend what happened, eyes fixed on the smoking fabric of the captain's jumpsuit, long enough for Thern, my friend and second, to fire his weapon at me.

I had enough time to feel the betrayal, the hurt, the confusion and the rage before the world blacked out, with the memory of the first female I'd had any genuine feelings for dying on the ground, along with the image of my oldest friend framed by the door to his bunk holding a kinetic gun in his hand.

Chapter 24

The clunks in my head reverberated throughout my whole being, spikes of pain that engulfed my body with each impact.

I was lying on the cold floor of my ship, the thrum of the engine not helping the headache. I couldn't remember how I came to be on the floor, why I was in pain, or why my chest felt numb.

But I recognized the voice coming from ahead: Ravi.

"...will pardon you. We can work this out."

A mocking laugh responded, and although it took me a few scary blank moments, I finally remembered.

Ravi asking me to wait before lifting the lockdown, walking with him to Thern's room and manually unlocking the door. The kinetic gun Thern had shot me with.

Motherfucker! Thern was the traitor. He was the traitor all along.

"I don't want a pardon," Thern said through gritted teeth.

I opened my eyes a fraction. Ravi sat a few meters away, his hands behind his back, no doubt bound. In front of him stood Thern, his back to me as he paced back and forth. On the corner, on the tactical seat, lay Sullivan, unconscious but breathing.

Why we were in the bridge I didn't know, but I wasn't ready to tip off Thern that I was awake.

"You can't kill the princess," Ravi snapped. "She's a child and heir to the throne. Damn it, Thern! How could you do this? My crew—your brothers-in-arms—my ship. The attack in Cyrus Station. You sold us out to the Voner pirates!"

Thern's fist flew. There was a loud crack and Ravi's face snapped to the side.

Splendor's Orbit

"I'm not doing this for me! I'm doing this for our people. Dolenta is a child and weak. The emperor is dying. The nobles are circling the throne like meat-peckers, searching for the moment they could strike and take over. They all think they're better than the other, and certainly better than the princess. We're facing a bloody revolution. The last time that happened, we destroyed an entire system!"

Ravi hissed. "You speak as if this is a done deal. The emperor is still alive, and even if he died today, Dolenta won't assume the throne for at least a decade. She'll have time to grow into her powers. Stars, Thern, she hasn't even been crowned."

"You refused her regency. You told the emperor to pick someone else."

"I don't want the power," Ravi said tightly.

"That's why I wanted you to have it. You won't abuse your position the way others would, and until then, we could have brainstormed something better."

"You mean a better coup?"

"She's a dowser," Thern said tiredly. "It doesn't matter how much her power grows, the people will never fear or respect her."

"Killing her is not going to make the problem go away."

Thern's exhale was slow and long. "I didn't want to kill her," he said with remorse. "Not the princess, not the *Wedva-Xa* crew. They were supposed to disable the ship, kidnap Dolenta, and take her somewhere where she could have lived her life safely. But they hit the *Wedva-Xa* early, and you kept thwarting all my arrangements."

"Did you pay the Human Confederacy too? Is that why the stealth ship downed their own?"

Thern snorted. "Blame me for everything but the pirates. I have nothing to do with that. Believe it or not, I wanted to spare everyone, but now we have no choice. If she dies, the emperor will have to invoke Moresy Cotelum. The nobility who believe themselves fit to rule will all join, along with the most powerful commoners."

"Moresy Cotelum hasn't been invoked in eight hundred years. It's antiquated, it's bloody, and it doesn't ensure a good ruler, only the most ruthless. Imagine a tyrant on the throne. Is that what you want? By the stars, Thern, imagine someone like Donnel ruling Krozalia."

"I have. It's why I'm here now, ensuring that the princess doesn't make it back. I can guarantee something fast and easy. Others won't be so kind. They'll drag out her suffering so the emperor capitulates faster."

"I can't let you do that. The emperor won't let you do that. Dying or not, he's still the most powerful person alive. Soon, the royal escorts will want to know why I'm not answering the comms, they'll figure something is wrong and board the ship. Even if they ignore the radio silence, we'll reach Dupilaz Moon in a few days. There's nothing you can do, no way for you to reach the princess."

I blinked at that. And then I realized why we were on the bridge. The lockdown. I'd never lifted it. A chill ran through my body. The only reason Thern hadn't killed the princess yet was because Dolenta was still locked in her bunk. I'd only used the override code for Thern—and he hadn't known that.

Thern sighed and shook his head, and his profile came into view. Just a brief glance, but enough for me to see the grief and regret in his eyes. That was when I knew.

Thern wasn't going to be dissuaded. He'd made up his mind and he was going to see this through. He couldn't lift the lockdown, but he could reach the rest of the ship and the engine room. If he had the right knowledge, which I assumed he did, he could tamper with the engines enough to cut off the air circulation or cause any number of incidents to explode the ship. He wasn't expecting to come out of this alive. By the way things had happened, the Class 5 Kroz Battleship, he hadn't meant to live through this.

He had nothing to lose.

Ravi must have realized the same thing. With a roar that would have made a savage proud, he threw himself at Thern.

Splendor's Orbit

Bound as he was and from his position, he could only tackle Thern's knees, but his second hadn't been expecting the move and both went down hard.

I told myself to move, to get up and stop Thern, but my body refused the command.

"Move, damn you," I hissed, inhaling a deep breath. The numbness on my right side should have frightened me, but most of that side was made of metal, and a few hours of rest should give my cybernetics time to restore whatever damage was taken—or, in a worst case scenario, a few hours with Baltsar and his tools.

Or so I told myself. I refused to consider anything else.

I did consider the fact that if I didn't get up and Thern won the fight, which he would, eventually, I'd be just as dead as everyone else on the ship.

So I made myself get up, first on all fours, then my knees, then to my feet. The world swayed a bit but steadied quickly enough. By then, Thern was atop Ravi, hands around his neck, choking him to death.

I looked around, but there was nothing to throw or hit Thern with. Plain fists, then. Or feet. My mag boots were sturdy and heavy enough to be considered weapons on their own. I raised my right, mechanical foot and kicked.

Thern threw himself sideways, so I only caught him on the shoulder, and then I was falling. Not because he had hit me or anything, but because my balance was still skewed.

I fell in front of Sullivan and met wide blue eyes. Sullivan was awake. Unfortunately, he was all tied up with some kind of wire.

Thern better not have pulled them from a console.

Sullivan began saying something, then his eyes shifted behind me. I threw myself sideways and kicked back, gratified at the grunt of pain when my foot connected.

But then a large hand wrapped around my leg and pulled so fast, my face grated on the floor.

"You're heavier than you look," he grunted, fisted my

hair, and pulled my head in an awkward angle that made it hard to swallow and breathe.

"I'm glad you're not dead," he murmured near my ear and pulled me upright, then touched something metal and sharp to my neck. "Don't," he said.

From the corner of my eye, I saw Ravi step away, hands still behind his back, eyes completely yellow.

"Good. I didn't mean for this to happen, and I'm sorry," he said. To whom, I didn't know, but he sounded sincere. "Please lift the lockdown." He thrust me at the pilot's seat and my console, though he kept a fist of my hair and the sharp tool close to my neck.

"No."

The sharp implement bit into my skin and a trickle of blood ran down my neck.

Ravi snarled. Sullivan cursed.

"Do it or I'll kill you," Thern said through gritted teeth.

"You're going to kill me anyway," I said and pressed forward. As I suspected, he pulled the knife away before it could cut deep, and I took that moment to snap my head back, stomp on his foot, and throw myself sideways.

Thern howled and let go of me, blade clacking on the floor. I grabbed it and dashed for Ravi. I must have miscalculated the strength of the stomp, or maybe Kroz warriors were immune to pain, because just as I reached Ravi, something like a giant fist punched me in the back, propelling me forward.

By the horror in Ravi's eyes and Sullivan's shout—and the ringing in my ears, Thern had just done something terrible to me. Something that caused my legs to go numb, and a red warning to flash in my right vision before it too, went dark.

Had Ravi's wrists been free, I was sure he'd have caught me, but as it was, he stumbled back with my weight, trying to prop me with his body by bending backward and lowering to the floor. I had held on to the knife and with my last remaining strength, used it to saw Ravi's bindings. I was sure I nicked him more than once.

The wire was nowhere near severed when I slid to the floor, face first, bells ringing in my ears and vision flashing—black and white, black and white.

"Void save us," Thern whispered above me. "She's a hypermorph."

It was that last statement, more than anything else that alarmed me.

Ravi shouted something just as a loud crack came and the wire that had bound his wrists snapped. Or maybe the wire snapped before he shouted something. I didn't know, the world was slowing down. A scuffle ensued somewhere on the other side of the bridge, but I was too out of it to pay attention. My upper body was burning like acid was eating through my veins, trying to mend itself even as the blood loss and the damage caused my vision to come and go out of focus. I was in shock, both from the injury and the fact that my darkest secret was revealed to the person who could, and would, demand my execution. I tried to breathe through it, only moving to avoid being trampled, the scuffle punctuated by grunts and curses. Dark pinpricks continuously appeared in my vision until finally, there was nothing but a sea of black.

Chapter 25

I awoke lying on my belly, in my bed. I was sore, groggy, but still alive. There was no confusion about what had happened and how events had unspooled on the bridge. My only questions were how I had gotten in bed and how much time had passed.

I inhaled, both lungs expanding with air. My fingers moved, all ten of them. So did my toes.

I opened my eyes next and found myself staring at the gray metal of the hull.

Now that I had determined that everything was working, I needed to find out the extent of the damage Thern had caused. To my body and whatever the effect of my exposure was.

It was at the dawn of space travel when humans began tinkering with the combination of human cloning and artificial intelligence. The idea had been to start an army of android clones, to reduce the loss of military personnel during wars. They weren't sentient beings then, but they might as well have been. With the abundance of knowledge and loopholes in their programming, it was only natural that the androids band together and began advocating for their rights. And then they turned the war around and started rioting. The human governments consolidated their knowledge to eradicate the problem, giving rise to the Human Confederacy.

Only, their problems, the android clones, were highly trained soldiers with the intelligence of warfare strategy at their fingertips. And so the android war began. It went on for months, with billions of human deaths, and the destruction of entire countries. Things would have continued going on had the Kroz not come to the human's aid. They fought and destroyed the android clones and set up the laws that banned genetic engineering, along with AI experimentations, on penalty of death.

But humans never learned from their mistakes, and here I was, a few centuries later, and a hypermorph—with a sentient AI to boot.

"Mac?" I said sub-vocally. The lack of response came as no surprise. Not when I could still feel the void in my psyche where his presence should have been.

A blurry image moved nearer, and I realized my right vision wasn't fully functioning yet. It wasn't as bad as it got when Baltsar disabled my cybernetics. Not ideal, but better than having half of my body disabled.

"What's the square root of 19321?" Ravi demanded in a gravelly voice.

"What?" I asked, confused.

I hadn't expected to wake up with him beside me, but I should have. The Grim Reaper of the galaxy wouldn't leave someone who'd broken one of the most sacred rules without keeping guard. The only reason I was alive still was probably because the *Splendor* was mostly in lockdown.

Sullivan came into view next. Of course. The CTF kept an eye out for anything that could bring Kroz Warriors knocking, and genetically enhancing humans was at the very top of the list.

I expected to find recrimination in Sullivan's eyes, maybe even hurt at what he no doubt perceived as a betrayal of my vow to uphold the law. Instead, I saw a carefully blank mask.

"Answer the question," Sullivan said.

I blinked. "What?"

"What's the square root of 19321?" Ravi repeated.

"Um. I don't know."

Feeling vulnerable, I moved to sit, wincing at the way my muscles protested and the sluggish response from my right side. It was clearly damaged, but considering I could still move and see, not as badly as I guessed.

I dropped my feet to the ground—bare of boots and

socks, then covered my bare legs as well. I had on a man's shirt, loose and buttoned from my thighs to my neck. In the back of my mind, I wondered if I'd been undressed so Ravi could determine how far my mechanics went, or if he had done it to strip me of any hidden weapons. Oddly enough, the sense of abused privacy stung more than it should, all things considered.

"We needed to see if there were any wounds that needed treatment," Sullivan explained, proving he still knew me well.

Ravi stepped fully into view, and I struggled to suppress my need to flee. For one, I'd never outrun him in my condition, and another, there was nowhere to go.

"He wouldn't let me put you in the med unit," Sullivan was saying. "So I did it the old-fashioned way."

"I already said this, human. She doesn't need it," Ravi intoned flatly.

"It would have helped her heal faster," Sullivan snapped, his mask breaking. He was furious. Whether that anger was for me or at me, I didn't know. Oddly enough, I didn't really care.

"If I wanted a katlicha zariva de re explosion on Drimovtry Tadiu for two hours straight, how much dovashka would I need?"

I stared at him uncomprehendingly for a few long seconds.

"How long does it take to travel from Sector 9 to Sector 2 with full FTL speed?"

"What are you doing?" I demanded. "Is this some kind of joke?"

His mouth tightened into a thin line and his eyes held a lifeless quality to them, as if he was a shell of a man instead of a breathing person. "Answer me."

"I don't know. I didn't even understand half of what you said." I dropped my eyes, unable to continue holding the indifference in his.

"Did you volunteer for the nanotech enhancement or did you pay to be modified?"

"Does it matter?"

Splendor's Orbit

"Answer. Me," Ravi bit out through gritted teeth.

Anger sparked inside me. "Neither," I spat, opening my arms wide to both sides. "I was taken against my will and experimented upon. Where were your enforcers then?"

The tension in my small cabin ratcheted up until the air was thick with it. I regretted my outburst the moment it had left my mouth. Whether I'd volunteered or not didn't change the outcome. I wished I'd found a way to leave V-5 without the Kroz, that I'd never taken this job. Then none of this would have happened. Not the Confederacy, not the fight with the Voners, not the discovery of my not-so-human status.

"When did this happen?" Sullivan asked, bringing my attention back to him.

I jerked a shoulder. "Why? There's nothing you can do about it."

"Who's Mac?" Ravi asked next.

I shook my head. "No one of your concern."

"You've spoken that name when unconscious."

"Still no one of your concern," I repeated coolly, meeting his eyes. None of the warmth I'd gotten accustomed to was there, replaced instead by cold indifference. The face of the galaxy's executioner.

I looked away.

"It was after the Genesis Mission, wasn't it?" Sullivan demanded. "The people who rescued you, they're the ones who did this. It's the reason why you never came back and let us know you survived."

"How many like you are out there?" Ravi questioned into the silence that followed Sullivan's statement.

"I don't know. None that I've been able to confirm, anyway."

"The lab where this happened, where is it? How many employees, how many subjects?"

"None." I raised my chin when Ravi's eyes flashed yellow with anger. "I killed them all, then destroyed the whole facility. I watched until it burned to ashes."

"Where and when?"

I sighed resignedly. "Raptune Planet, Sector 8. In the Ferhos Land near the desert nine years ago."

"How much control does the AI have over you?"

"Hold up a minute," Sullivan said. "That's a big leap from bioengineering to AI synchronization."

Ravi ignored Sullivan's outburst. "How much?"

"None," I said. It wasn't a lie. Mac and I were two separate consciousnesses.

Ravi glanced down, and for the first time, I saw the small device he held in his hands.

"What's that?"

Ravi raised his head and met my eyes. "A hypermorph detector."

My mouth went dry. I hadn't known such devices existed, but it made sense that if one was there, the Kroz would have it. How else could they enforce the law?

"What does it say?"

Without answering, he pocketed the device and turned to leave. "Please release the lockdown. It's been more than twenty-six hours."

"What are you going to do to me?" I asked his back.

Ravi stopped by the door. He didn't turn around, but I could have sworn he looked defeated. "You saved the princess' life more than once. I can't make a decision about you on my own." With that said, he left, the door sliding shut with a low hiss.

I frowned down at my clenched fists. Dread and disappointment ate at me, the latter more potent than it ought to be, considering what had just happened. I shouldn't have been disappointed. Even if he hadn't found out my secret, we were days away from parting, never to see each other again.

But I had hoped for more, I thought, recalling the chaste brush of his lips on mine. I'd wanted more.

I exhaled slowly, an involuntary release of the breath I'd been holding.

"Clara," Sullivan began slowly. "Was the Genesis Facility tinkering with bioengineering and AI's synchronization?"

I considered lying, but the troubled look in his eyes gave me pause. "What do you know?" I asked first. There was something—knowing in the question.

He raked a hand through his hair, the strands longer than they had been when we started this journey. "This is confidential CTF business, but seeing you're still a soldier and a captain, I'm not breaking my oath." He licked his lips, clearly nervous, and a strange feeling began growing in the pit of my stomach. Something like unease, only stronger. I wasn't going to like this.

"A few years ago, we were returning from a mission on this small Cradox planet on the edges of Sector 9 when we were attacked. The fight was intense, and we took heavy hits, but we compromised their ship and they couldn't stop us from boarding and taking them prisoners.

"There were three of them. They were all Cradoxian teenagers. Kids who were born and raised on the Inner Planets. Clara—Leann—they were all hypermorphs with sentient AIs in control of their actions."

"Did they say anything? The Cradoxian officials?"

A haunting look darkened the baby blue of his eyes. "They self-destroyed the moment the interrogators discovered they were hypermorphs. If the researchers hadn't already taken blood and tissue samples, we wouldn't have found out their real identities from before."

"And their government?"

"We never inquired about anything. We figured they were building an army to overthrow the CTF, and so we sent in spies to monitor their doings. Nothing concrete was ever found, and now I'm wondering if it's because the Cradoxian hypermorphs were just the victims of some other secret lab."

The "human" wasn't added to that last word, but it was implied. I looked down at my hands, trying to process Sullivan's information with what I knew. If the scientists were experimenting on other races as well, did that mean those scientists weren't all humans either?

Baltsar isn't, but he's passing as one. His alien half wasn't public knowledge, but something he preferred keeping under wraps. Maybe the people who'd employed him had known from the start about his mixed-race heritage.

Aware that Sullivan was still waiting for an answer to his question, I decided to give him something he could use, something he could investigate in the likely event that I didn't make it out of this alive.

"They tried implanting a sentient AI in my brain," I said quietly. "They'd have succeeded too had one of the technicians not been newly employed and unaware of the clandestine work. He helped me fake the programming, risking his own life in the process. I was too weak and disoriented to fight or run—it took months for me to master my cybernetics. When the time came, he helped me kill all the scientists and destroyed the facility."

"Who's he? The CTF would—"

"Never know he exists," I said fiercely. "I'll not repay his help by throwing him into the flames. He saved my life, Sunny. I won't reward that by ratting him out when all he wants is to live his life in solitude."

The silence that followed my words was strained, filled with unspoken demands. Maybe Sullivan saw the determination in my eyes; maybe he understood he'd never pry the knowledge from me.

He exhaled, shoulders slumping. "I'm sorry," he said, clasping my cold fist in his warm hand and squeezing. "You know we'd have searched the galaxy for you if we'd known."

A hard lump of emotion clogged my throat, and I opened my hand and squeezed his back. "I know."

"Is Alex out there, too?"

"No. He didn't make it through the implants."

Sullivan's mouth pinched. "I don't know if I should be thankful for that or not," he said quietly. "We left you two there, easy pickings to the vultures."

Splendor's Orbit

I had nothing to say to that. I reached for the drawer of the stand and grabbed a protein bar. I finished four before I started feeling better.

"I should lift the lockdown before Ravi loses his shit waiting."

Sullivan stood at once. "I'll give you privacy to dress," he said and made for the door.

I stood, made sure my legs held under my weight, and headed into the adjacent head to clean up.

The first thing I did was check the injury that had given me away. I unbuttoned the shirt, again feeling the disorientation and resentment of being stripped while I was unconscious. Both feelings gave way to curiosity at the discoloration covering my chest. I touched the bruise gingerly, wincing as I recalled being shot with Thern's kinetic gun sometime before I'd awoken on the bridge. Then I turned my back to the mirror and craned my neck. There, between my spine and right shoulder blade, a fist-sized red puckered wound. It was closed, but it was the size of my fist, so it must have been a horrific wound. I shrugged my shoulder, biting back a gasp of pain as the metal casing for my mechanical right shoulder appeared, just a small flash, but there nonetheless. Had the shot hit me a bit to the left, I might not have made it, fast healing or no.

Thern had meant to kill me with that second shot. The realization clenched my insides. And I hadn't escaped that fate yet.

The fingers of my right hand wiggled, an involuntary response to the injury that should have killed me, or caused mobility difficulty in the very least. As it was, repairing the skin and whatever else that had been damaged would take some time yet. I wondered if there would be a need for mechanical repairs too. There was nothing I could do about that now, here, so far from Baltsar and his tools.

Clean, refreshed, hydrated, and as presentable as possible, I entered the bridge. Ravi and Sullivan were both there; the former in the co-pilot's seat, the latter in the tactical chair.

Without a word, I slid into the pilot's seat and began the process of lifting the lockdown. I wanted to ask Ravi what would happen to me, what he meant about not being able to decide my fate on his own, what the options were and if I had any say. Instead, I kept my silence.

***

The mood in the galley was dark, with undertones of anger whenever I caught Ravi's or Lorenzo's eyes. Both were simmering with rage, marinating whatever thoughts crossed their minds, not voicing anything out loud. Ravi, because he probably didn't want knowledge of what had happened to spread, Lorenzo because he was no doubt concocting something nasty to pay me back for keeping the lockdown more than a day after the danger was over.

Dolenta and Cassandra asked after Thern, but Ravi deflated the curiosity by saying he'd received some bad news and wouldn't be joining us. I could tell Dolenta wasn't satisfied with the answer but didn't press the point. No doubt she was accustomed to keeping her thoughts to herself.

Everyone was hungry, so lunch was a simple vegetable casserole that Ravi had prepared. I hadn't expected him to want to cook, but I should have. He had, for the whole voyage, prepared at least one meal a day.

I ate quickly, set my plate in the sanitizer, and left, expecting to hear Mac's voice in my ear, my heart sinking when it didn't come. There was a void in my head where he should have been, scooped out with all the energy I'd spent hopping the *Splendor* to safety.

Not that saving the Kroz had done me any good. This journey might still have a fatal outcome, at least for me.

Footsteps approached the bridge, pausing by the open door. I braced myself, expecting it to be Ravi, so I was surprised when Sullivan spoke.

"May I come in?"

I glanced back and frowned. "Sure."

He stepped in, looking at the control panels, the console,

the screens, hands stuffed in his pockets.

"Spit it out, man," I said.

"It's nothing," he began, meeting my steady eyes and sighing. "I just wanted you to know that I understand why you never called. Why you never let us know you were alive."

"It was kinder and safer for everyone," I answered honestly.

He exhaled sharply, raked a hand over his short hair, and said nothing else. There was some gray scattered near his temples, proof that he was aging while I wasn't. Cassandra was right. I hadn't changed in the decade since they'd seen me last. While I could claim good genes now, I wouldn't be able to in a few more years. It was another reason I'd "remained dead" and something I'd need to figure out what to do about. Reconstructive medicine was an option I could use in a pinch, but it wouldn't be a solution either, not without rousing suspicion.

If I escaped this voyage alive, I'd be setting up a meeting with Leo for a new identity. It would suck to start again from scratch, but that was the beauty of a vast galaxy and a good forger: Leo could create a background that would be hard to prove fake, as long as I set up in another colony. A new sector would be even better. Sector 7, maybe. There were human colonies in the Brofil system, and even if I settled outside that, I wouldn't look out of place. Brofils appeared human, with their slightly longer canines and the blue tint to their skins the only difference to humans.

Besides, their laws were looser than the laws in other sectors.

Lorenzo stomped in while I contemplated my future, and by the triumphant glint in his eyes, I knew he'd come up with the best payback for keeping him locked up.

"Captain Colderaro," he began.

"Lee. It's Captain Lee."

His upper lip curled at the corner in disgust. "Captain Colderaro, since our stealth ships were destroyed, I'm commandeering your ship for our return journey. From now until we are back in Confederacy Space, you're no longer the captain of this ship."

I was up, right hand around his throat, the left fisting a bunch of his jumpsuit before he'd finished the last word. I thumped him against the wall and snarled. "You're not. Going. To fucking. Touch. My ship." With every word, I thumped him harder. Lorenzo's face was reddening fast, both the result of the raging anger I could see in his eyes and the lack of oxygen.

It was Sullivan who came to Lorenzo's aid. "Clara!" Sullivan grabbed my wrist but didn't try pulling me off. His voice was in my ear, soothing and nonsensical. But it brought me back to reality, and the fact I had Lorenzo by the throat, pinned against the wall with one hand, and that his feet weren't even touching the ground. I let go and slumped back into Sullivan, who quickly pulled me away with one arm around my middle and the other still holding my right wrist.

Lorenzo was rubbing his neck, the imprint of my fingers red and clear on his skin. At the door stood Ravi, blank mask in place that had me actually thinking about the consequences of my actions. Not by the Kroz—they already had enough on me for an execution—but by the CTF. I wasn't supposed to have enough strength to grab a grown man by the neck one-handed and pull him off his feet. Hell, had Lorenzo been a few inches taller, I wouldn't have been able to pull it off on account of I wasn't tall enough for that. I had no doubt that tidbit would be making it into Lorenzo's next report—once he stopped long enough to wonder about it. At the moment, rage had him practically foaming at the mouth. He advanced on me, hatred shooting from his eyes like sparks off short-circuiting cables.

Ravi cleared his throat, and Lorenzo's gaze shifted to the side. For a moment, I could see him weighing the pros and cons of attacking me in the presence of the Kroz.

"We will discuss this again after I see our guests off," he said to me and turned.

"Actually," Ravi began mildly, "Captain Lee will be

accompanying us down to Krozalia. The emperor has asked to meet her in person."

I wondered if that was a euphemism for execution. A meeting where I'd accidentally, and tragically, meet my death.

"Of course," Lorenzo said smoothly. "We'll extend our stay for another week."

"No."

Lorenzo opened his mouth again, but Ravi cut him off. "Captain Lee's visit will be for an undetermined period."

"I'm afraid we can't do that," Lorenzo said. "Surely you understand. Our mission was to have you reach your destination safely, and you'd introduce me to the Kukona mineral trading committee on Dupilaz Moon. We've done the former and you refuse to finalize the latter. My superiors won't tolerate us delaying this journey with nothing to show for it."

Ravi inclined his head. "I understand your dilemma. That's why I've arranged an escort for you back to Cyrus Station."

Lorenzo sputtered. "We can't leave without Captain Colderaro now that we've lost both stealth ships protecting your princess."

I winced. But that only proved to me that Lorenzo didn't know about Blackbird's treachery. Ravi's expression iced over and the temperature in the bridge lowered a few degrees. In that instance and for the first time since I'd laid eyes on him in the market at V-5, I could see the Grim Reaper in the Kroz across from Lorenzo.

I was certain then that Ravi was going to show him the recording of Blackbird firing on Eagle 13, but once again he proved my expectations wrong.

"If you're concerned about your journey's safety without Captain Lee's battle skills, I assure you, my men are more competent than ten of your stealth fighters put together. The Kroz value the lives of our warriors. I will personally guarantee your safety back home."

Lorenzo straightened, the realization that he wasn't going

to win this flicking in his expression. "No, no. There's no need for that. I'll talk to command and let them know we're being delayed. Maybe we can even renegotiate a deal for the Kukona minerals. It's only fitting that we be compensated for our time and losses too."

"I already told you, human. There will be no KKM trade with the Confederacy."

"You've said that. But it's my understanding that you're not in charge of trade in Krozalia. If you can arrange a meeting with the interested parties, we can extend our stay in Krozalia."

Ravi's jaw clenched and his gaze lowered to the imprint of my fingers on Lorenzo's neck as if he was contemplating finishing the job himself. But then he surprised me by agreeing. "Very well. I'll give you the chance to speak with the Minister of Foreign Trade and Development. But I promise nothing more."

Chapter 26

Lord Drax

I stared down at the dark square in my hand, feeling hollow. Such a small, ordinary object. So deceptive.

I hadn't lied when I told Captain Lee it was a hypermorph detector. But I hadn't told her that had it identified her as one, this small box would have sent her the equivalent of ten lightning bolts and disrupted any signals she might have had. It would have been the end of the captain, the shy smiles, and the vibrant energy she carried.

Something inside me had withered away when I was waiting in her bunk with the knowledge that I was ready to end her existence. I closed my fist, crushing the box. I ignored the zing it gave me and dropped the broken remains.

I wanted to believe that I knew the box wouldn't have activated, that I hadn't been prepared to end her. That the captain wasn't a hypermorph, regardless of her fast healing and cybernetic enhancements. It had always been said that hypermorphs had no aura, and Leann's was as bright as a star's. But I hadn't known. Each moment that had dragged while I stood there watching her injuries stitch together, my doubt had tormented me. Technology was always advancing, and although I couldn't see when or how, there was the possibility that someone had found a way to create a hypermorph with an aura.

An image of the fist-sized hole in Leann's back flashed in my mind. The way the blood had clotted and how the titanium plates had slid, almost as if sentient, to close the wound. But it was the traces of Kukona mineral zigzagging through the titanium plates that had made my blood run cold.

The need to shout my rage to the galaxy swelled inside me and lodged in my throat, like a fist-sized block that made it hard to breathe. Not only had my friend and second-in-command conspired against the crown, but the female who'd roused my interest was genetically enhanced. The person who could possibly be the other half of a life bond, a connection few Kroz were blessed to have.

I let my chin drop and my body sagged with defeat. I might have been able to prevent the captain's execution, but the emperor wouldn't ignore the implications of what the KKM in her enhancements meant.

The humans were growing bolder. As evidenced by the captain, they were now kidnapping able soldiers believed to be dead in action to experiment on. Somewhere out there was a lab with enough knowledge to create hypermorphs. Whether Captain Lee was the first, the last, or just an experiment meant nothing. The knowledge was out, and so was all the equipment to simulate the perfect environment for their creation. Even if the Captain had claimed to have destroyed the lab, I could see she hadn't been telling the entire truth.

I remembered when, some years ago, we received a tip about a facility experimenting with enhancements. I remembered back then, we hadn't been sure which race was behind it. The tip had been anonymous, but the evidence had been undeniable. Maybe we'd misread them—maybe the evidence hadn't been for an enhancement lab, but a hypermorph one.

It had taken a few months and another tip about a lab between Sector 8 and Sector 9 for us to narrow it down. We'd resorted to sending both the humans and the Cradoxians dire warnings. The Confederacy had been the first to deny having any knowledge.

But now I knew. They had lied. Whether they'd done it on purpose or had been ignorant of the happenings in their own Sector was the question that would decide their fate. I dusted my hand off the remnant of the hypermorph detector and stood. It was time for the Confederacy to start rooting out their illegal labs, or the Kroz would take control of their government and do it for them.

What no one knew was that the Kroz had already fought a war against hypermorphs—or sentient AIs—and had unique knowledge of the devastation they could cause. After all, Sector 1, the Kroz's first home system, had been obliterated in that war, over a millennium ago.

Our history was riddled with strife, but none had scarred the Kroz more than the Hypermorph War. Kroz warriors were dispersed throughout the galaxy, on the lookout for signs of genetic manipulation—the first step to creating a hypermorph—their sole duty the up keeping of that law.

Each year, genetically modified individuals were brought to Krozalia for public execution. Sometimes one, sometimes two. Three at the most. I had never had any trouble ending their lives.

I forced myself to picture Leann on the execution platform, forced myself to imagine the buildup of energy ready to snuff her from existence. Of their own volition, my thoughts shifted—Leann behind her flimsy stand selling used ship parts, gray eyes watching me warily. The irritated look she'd given me on Cyrus Station when she confronted me about following her. The fierce look of concentration in her face as she focused on her console, biting her lower lip. The hurt she'd tried to conceal when I had interrogated her after Thern's betrayal. The rare smiles reserved for Dolenta. The kindness and compassion she offered the princess during their interactions. My breath caught in my throat as recognition hit. Captain Leann Smith was in no danger from me. Magic flared through my veins, crackling like lightning. I wanted, no, needed her to be safe, to thrive. The great duty-bound passion that I was familiar with, the one that had always flamed to protect the Princess and my people, ignited in me. But this time, it burned for Leann. And it raged with a fervor I'd never tasted. I wanted to be her protector, her shield, her calm through violent storms.

The revelation stunned me in its intensity. Never before had I felt such an overpowering urge to safeguard another being. I swallowed as my hands trembled. I couldn't deceive myself. This was no mere desire to protect. It was a soul-deep yearning to cherish.

Chapter 27

There would be no stopping on Dupilaz Moon. Now that Ravi had made sure I'd be going to Krozalia, he opted to complete this last leg of the journey aboard the *Splendor*.

With Thern's betrayal still fresh, I couldn't help but agree. How many other trusted friends had thrown their lot with Thern "for the greater good of Krozalia?" There was no need to risk getting caught by Thern's supporters—especially since he had no doubt sent word that Dupilaz Moon would be our stop.

Lorenzo and Cassandra had asked after Thern a few times, Cassandra with concern, Lorenzo with suspicion. The princess seemed to have accepted that Thern wouldn't be joining us for meals anymore. Whether because Ravi had explained things to her or because she was accustomed to taking the word of her elders at face value, I didn't know.

Mac had yet to come back online, though I'd run several diagnostics tests and troubleshooting. Cassandra had also checked all the engines for any damage—not that she was aware of Mac. But nothing was wrong. Not with the ship, not with Mac's core program. The motherboard in my wrist looked fine, and no amount of reset brought his voice back. Everything else in the ship was working, save for the pathetically low charge that I was beginning to wonder would take months to replenish. Cassandra was confident the ship would be half-charged before long, but I had my doubts.

Lucky for me, Lorenzo behaved himself, though each time I crossed his line of sight, hatred oozed from him like the noxious fumes of V-5's Waste Management Facilities. Considering I kept to the bridge and my bunk, exposure to his hatred wasn't much. But I still had to eat and I refused to be driven from my own galley.

Ten days after Thern's betrayal, we entered Krozalia's orbit. The planet had been constantly growing on the port view screen, now filling it with vivid blues and lush greens and all shades in the color spectrum. It was bigger than any planet I'd ever been to, the only one that was habitable in this entire sector of the galaxy.

With the background of brilliant stars and the blue-white cloud of a nebula stretching like phantom fingers, the scene outside the ship was the dream of every poet and painter. Literally, I thought, recalling some pictures I'd seen in history books.

But reality surpassed every depiction I'd seen.

"It's beautiful, isn't it?" Ravi asked from right behind me.

I flinched, not having heard his approach. My enhancements weren't functioning to full capacity yet, as proven by the constant trembling and lack of strength in my right hand. Even so, I hadn't expected how off guard I was when I should have been on full alert.

Mac would have never let anyone come so close without warning me. Especially someone clearly in the enemy zone.

I turned, catching the tightness around his eyes and mouth before they smoothed into a stoic mask.

"Yes," I said honestly. "I've never seen anything like it before."

"Weren't you born on a planet?"

A curious glint shone in his eyes as if the details of my birth were a fascinating topic.

"Yes. Nebula Val. My family owns a freight company there." I saw no reason why I should lie, considering he already knew the dangerous parts.

"So you're following the family trade."

I shrugged. "It's something I know how to do."

"Yes, and do well."

Splendor's Orbit

I gave him a sideways look, but the offhand compliment seemed genuine. It made me uncomfortable, a mix of emotions swirling within me—fear of what the Kroz would do to me, what the Confederacy had planned, Mac's absence, and the dread that my future was out of my hands.

I stood, unable to keep myself seated and in a vulnerable position, and found myself standing too close to Ravi. Close enough that the smell of cinnamon and smoke and his unique musk flooded my senses.

"Will my execution be publicized?" I blurted out when he didn't move.

I hadn't meant to voice the question, but his closeness compelled me to speak, and the uncertainty had been eating at me. It wasn't that I cared what people thought of me, or would be there to feel any of the humiliation of such a public event, but...my family believed me dead in action, not a disgraced fugitive who'd been caught and now served as a cautionary tale for other law-breaking individuals.

I'd never been close to my family. As the eldest child in Confederacy Space, my conscription to the army had been a done deal even as a fetus in my mother's womb. I'd been cared for, educated, given all the comforts and material luxury my family could buy—and they could buy a lot. But the warmth and affection my brother and sister were given had never been given to me. In a way, I'd had more freedom, my needs and every want met. It was how my parents made up for knowing my time in the family was limited.

And I'd always resented that, the clear separation that had marked me as different, even if I'd understood my parents had no say about my future. Yet, I'd rather have them believe me dead in a mission gone wrong than executed for breaking the galaxy's most sacred rule.

To my family, I was just another casualty sent out to enforce the Confederacy laws. A common enough event. Most firstborns never returned, and those who did were never able to fit back in, having done and seen too many horrors to fit again into their social mold.

"You're not going to be executed," Ravi said in a low, dangerous voice.

Startled at the words and the intensity of his tone, I glanced up and found umber eyes blazing—too close. I tried to step back, coming flush with the back of the pilot's seat.

Throat tightening and heart pounding, I asked, "What, then?"

There were few rules enforced galaxy-wide. Genetic manipulation and hypermorphs featured at the top of the forbidden list. Torture was a possibility, but to what end? I didn't know who held the scientists' strings. If I had, I'd have already gone after them.

"No one is going to kill you," he repeated, eyes fierce, as he closed the small gap between us. "I won't let anyone harm you."

I swallowed, mouth dry. My breathing turned shallow and sweat dotted my upper lip.

"Fear not, Leann." He touched a hand to my cheek, then traced warm fingers past my ear and into my hair. The pressure he put there was minimal but unmistakable.

My heart was racing so fast; I was having trouble breathing. I had no idea what he thought he was doing—until he lowered his face to mine.

"What-what are you doing?" I stammered, feeling a fine tremor coursing down my spine.

"I'd like to kiss you," he said bluntly, and again put some pressure on the back of my neck.

My eyes lowered to his mouth, the contour of his lips, the perfect bow on the bottom, and the subtle dip on the top.

"Unless you'd rather not?"

My eyes shot up to his, and flames engulfed my cheeks. There were greens and oranges and sparks of grey in his eyes, the slit pupils no longer jarring.

"Yes?" Ravi prompted. Just one word…with the potential to change everything.

Splendor's Orbit

"Yes," I murmured.

The yellow flared a second before Ravi slanted his mouth over mine, hungry and possessive. Electricity zinged through my entire system, igniting my nerve endings. The back of my chair pressed against my back while Ravi's entire body boxed me in. Oddly, the idea that I was trapped and at his mercy only made me crave more. I made a sound low in my throat, and suddenly Ravi stepped away.

"I am sorry," he said, not looking at me.

"Don't be." I reached for him, hand curving around his bicep. He didn't bend or close the gap again, seeming to hold his breath, blank mask in place. But I'd seen his desire, felt the hunger in his kiss. It emboldened me when I'd have otherwise second-guessed my action. I put some pressure on his arm, just a hint as I raised to the tip of my toes. For a moment he resisted, long enough for the cold realization of embarrassment to make me let go quickly, ready to step back and flee the bridge. But then he swooped in, one arm circling around my back and pulling me close as his mouth closed over mine, hot and insistent. The swipe of his thumb below my ear made me weak, my knees buckled, and my brain short-circuited.

I had no idea for how long we kissed, my mind blank of thoughts, all my senses focused on Ravi, his lips, the strong beat of his heart against mine, the heat trail of his wandering hands.

Gone was the shy warrior who thought it inappropriate to be in my bunk while I had lain in my bed, replaced by a demanding man with a scorching mouth.

By the time he pulled away, I was gasping for air, my legs weak and trembling. His arm around my waist was the only thing keeping me upright.

We stood facing each other, less than a hand's width apart, breathing each other's air. And then he let go of me and stepped away. He rubbed at his chest, looking shocked. "I'm sorry. We shouldn't have done that."

"Please," I said, not sure exactly what I was begging him for and not caring how low that brought me.

"I'm sorry." It was the apology and regret in his voice and eyes—like twin icepicks—that broke through the warm haze cocooning me, shattering whatever insanity I'd been spelled under. I flinched and stumbled back.

"No. Don't do that," he said and took a step closer. His eyes softened. "We shouldn't have done that, not because I think it's wrong, but because I need a clear head for what's coming." He touched the back of his knuckles to my cheek and searched my eyes. "I don't regret this and fully intend to explore this thing between us. But I can't—we shouldn't—not now with so much at stake."

"Like my life?"

"No. Never your life. No one is going to hurt you. I'll make sure of that."

He must have read my doubt because he lowered his forehead to mine and closed his eyes for a few seconds before opening them again. He uttered a string of lyrical words in Krozalian that had hints of promises and poetry, and I never wished for a translator more than I did at that moment.

"What does it mean?" I asked.

"As long as I live, as long as I have breath, your protection and safety are my duties to keep. On my life, my soul, I swear this."

I swallowed a hard lump. I didn't think that was a loosely given vow. "I don't want you getting hurt because of me."

Ravi huffed, his breath fanning my face. He let go, stepped back, then turned to leave. "I'll do more than that if it means protecting you." Then he left, and I stood there, anxious and nervous because I knew even if he accepted what I was, not everyone would.

I stood there for a long time, long enough for my legs to cramp and my heart to stop pounding. Then I fell back into the pilot's seat, feeling lighter than when I'd awoken, hopeful even, despite the fact that I knew whatever lay ahead, it was out of my hands. But I was alive, and as long as that remained true, I'd tackle the obstacles as they came my way, one at a time.

Splendor's Orbit

I bit my lip and savored the lingering taste of Ravi's kisses. What lay ahead was unknown, Mac was still offline, but the princess was safe, Ravi was on my side, and Thern had been dealt with.

With blooming hope in my chest, I strapped in and began preparing the *Splendor* for gravity.

"Prepare for landing," I announced in the coms. "We'll enter atmospheric pressure in five minutes."

With my focus on the gorgeous planet rapidly approaching, I knew my life was going to change drastically.

My future might not be looking certain, but at least it was looking gorgeous. Whether it would be gorgeous and dangerous, gorgeous and deadly, or gorgeous and adventurous, or even all three had yet to be determined.

And for the first time in a long time, I was actually looking forward to it.

***

Captain Lee's journey continues on *Imperial Stardust (The MacLee Chronicles book 2)*

I love to chat with readers, so if you'd like to say hi, ask questions, engage with other readers, or be the first to know about new releases and sales, come join my group https://www.facebook.com/groups/5454200234675036

Subscribe to my newsletter to be the first to know about new releases, read excerpts, and receive updates on my writing.

Jina S. Bazzar

Character and Glossary List (in alphabetic order)

Admiral Fulk: (human) high-ranking official for the CTF.

Alex Rubin: (human) co-pilot for the CTF.

Ashak: gland responsible for the storing and the channeling of Kroz magic, located near the vocal chords.

Bloyer Muz: (Cradox) Control Tower Supervisor on Station V-5.

Brofil: alien race native to Sector 7. They live on a blood-based diet and look human, save for a blue tinge to their skin.

Captain Elias: (human) captain of the stealth ship Eagle 13.

Captain Jacobs: (race unspecified) captain of the Black Court—located on Cyrus Station.

Captain Sullivan, AKA Sunny: (human) captain for the Confederacy Task Force.

Cassandra, AKA Cassie: (human) system's engineer for the CTF.

Centaur's Gateway: closest gateway to Cyrus Station—goes from Sector 8 to Sector 7 and vice versa.

Cheche: small furry rodents native to Cyrus Station.

Commodore Lorenzo: (human) commodore for the CTF.

Cradox: alien race native to Sector 9. Some are humanoid in shape, others are insectile. They've been warring with humans from Sector 8 for decades.

CTF: (human military) Confederacy Task Force, responsible for Sector 8.

Cyrus Station: station at the mid-point between two

major gateways. Ruled by the Obsidian Court.

Dante's Gateway: gateway at the edge of Sector 8, close to Sector 9.

Dradja: person oath-sworn to protect someone at the cost of their own life.

Donnel: (Kroz) high-ranking official in the Krozalian government.

Felicia, AKA Dolenta Tsakid: (Kroz) Krozalian princess and future empress.

HSA: Human Supreme Assembly—the human representative body for all the major space stations and colonies. Located on Earth and comprised of seven members, one from each Earth continent.

Leann Smith, AKA Clara Colderaro: (human) once a captain for the CTF and now captain of her own ship, the *Splendor*.

Leo: (race unspecified) hacker, Leann's informant.

Mac: sentient AI embedded in Leann's wrist.

Meat-peckers: carrion birds native to Krozalia.

Moresy Cotelum: ancient and violent competition put in place to determine the next Krozalian ruler in the event the royal family has no heir left.

Obsidian Court: ruling body of Cyrus Station.

Ravi Drax, AKA Madrovi Fidraxi: (Kroz) Krozalia's head guard, the emperor's left hand, and the Grim Reaper of the Galaxy.

Rodona Gateway: gateway on Sector 5—Krozalian System.

Rokoskiv Tsakid: (Kroz) emperor of Krozalia, Dolenta's father, purportedly the most powerful person in the galaxy.

Salba: small uninhabitable planet near V-5 Station.

Thern Boloski: (Kroz) Ravi's second in command.

V-5 Station: artificial space station between Sector 8 and 9.

Voner: space pirates.

Wedva-Xa: translated to Dark Sky. Ravi's personal ship,

near V-5 in an ambush.

Acknowledgments

It's that time again, and I've never been more thankful to everyone who has helped me finish, yet again, another book.
To the beta readers—Louis, Holly, Amy, Alex, and Courtney—thank you for all your feedback and insights, and for letting me bounce ideas whenever I was stuck. To Sally, your cheerful feedback always gave me the best vibes about Leann and this story.
To Tania and the team at MiblArt, for all your patience in designing my gorgeous covers.
To authors E. Denise Billups and Tyler Colins, for being there since the beginning, all these years ago.
To my kids, for not batting an eyelash even when I was making no sense.
And lastly, but never the least, thank you, the reader. You give me the strength to continue writing even when I'm at my wit's end.

Jina S. Bazzar

Other books by Jina S. Bazzar

The MacLee Chronicles
Splendor's Orbit 1
Imperial Stardust 2
Eclipsed Crown 3
Shadow Walker Series
Shadow Walker 1
Shadow Pawn 2
Shadow Flames 3
Shadow War 4
The Roxanne Fosch Files
Heir of Ashes 1
Heir of Doom 2
Heir of Fury 3
The Curse (A Roxanne Fosch Files Novella)
The Archives of Innah McLeod
Crimson Spellscape 1
The Grosh Alliance 2 (coming summer 2024)
From Fame to Ruin: A Gripping Standalone Romantic Suspense Novel

About the author

Jina Bazzar is a Palestinian author, born and raised in Brazil. Like most writers, her love of books began at a young age. Unlike most writers, she never aspired to become one.

It was only years after she became blind that she tried her hand at writing, giving voice to all the wild, rambling thoughts in her mind.

She now lives in Palestine with her family, taking inspiration from the smallest things in life. When she's not writing or networking on social media, you can find her in the kitchen, baking while listening to (often very loud) music.

Printed in Great Britain
by Amazon